Book II

Pillars of Matchstick Men

Pillars of Matchstick Men

Pillars of Matchstick Men

Book II

A.K. Baxter

A.K. Baxter

The Nine Realms series are stand-alone books and are a work of fiction. Names, places, characters and events are all created by the author's imagination and do not resemble real people living or dead. Locations and public sites used are created for the story alone and any resemblance of places, people, or things are coincidental.

Copyright©2019 by A.K. Baxter

All Rights reserved. No part of this book may be used or reproduced in any form, digital, electronic, mechanical, including photocopying and recording, unless specifically contracted for audio books or legitimate reviewing purpose, without the prior written permission of the publisher:

Mount Willow Books: mountwillowbooks@mail.com

Canada

A.K. Baxter

Library and Archives Canada Cataloguing in Publication

Front cover design and Illustrations by Ariane' Kamps:

linktr.ee/cloverpullover

Middle Grade Fantasy Novel

Nine Realms: Pillars of Matchstick Men, Book II

Issued in print and electronic formats

ISBN: 978-1-7752053-4-0 (PRINT)

ISBN: 978-1-7752053-5-7 (E-BOOK)

Printed in USA

First Edition: January 2019

Pillars of Matchstick Men

DEDICATION

I would like to dedicate this book to all the littles in my life, Elsie, Rowan, Evelyn, Patrick, Charlie and Suki.

Watching you all grow gives me such great pleasure. I hope the magic within these pages lives on, and inspires you to believe in all things magic and mystical.

Cherish our planet, our friendships and family.

For Magic Lies Within, Never Without.

Pillars of Matchstick Men

ACKNOWLEDGMENTS

To Ariane' Kamps, for your miraculous artistic skills in bringing my characters and universe to life.

To Sandy, for your input and marrying such a wonderful artist.

To all BETA readers and editors for your support and critique throughout.

Table of Contents

The Nine Realms	10
Chapter 0	12
Chapter 1	14
Chapter 2	27
Chapter 3	38
Chapter 4	52
Chapter 5	66
Chapter 6	79
Chapter 7	92
Chapter 8	101
Chapter 9	111
Chapter 10	116
Chapter11	129
Chapter 12	140
Chapter 13	152
Chapter 14	164

A.K. Baxter

A.K. Baxter

The Nine Realms

- ❖ A universe with its own gravitational laws, connected by thoughts and energy. Each realm home to the creatures and beings of whole.

- ❖ The Guardian Realm: home to the spirits, ancestors, shamans, spirit animals, and occasionally the tooth faeries.

- ❖ The Angelic Realm: home to the elves and the elders.

- ❖ The Magna Realm: or you may know it as the mythology realm, of all things wonderful, including dragons, and gods of old and new.

Pillars of Matchstick Men

- ❖ Intrepidus Gorge: Beholds the giants, ogres, and trolls. Creatures feared on a Journey through mirrors, to reveal their healed souls, as pure as the elves.

- ❖ Turner Realm: Within the underworld, home to the likes of werewolves, vampires, shapeshifters and naguals.

- ❖ Kingdom of Healers: We are all connected to this kingdom—even you, but only those creatures that pursue a life of healing reside here, like the dwarfs, animals and trees.

- ❖ The Faery Realm: Protectors of nature live among those tricky pixies and the brownies.

- ❖ The Human Realm: Home to the Goboids and Earthlings. All creatures wander through this realm and their own, freely, yet discreetly.

Chapter 0

Many moons have eclipsed my wings since we last met. Even the source's messenger needs a rest and as time grows near to my rebirth, my wings grow weary and my fire flares. A holiday to nestle is where this story begins. As a Phoenix on the breath of wind and birth of fire, I am sure you'd agree it would be difficult to travel your world without being seen.

Pillars of Matchstick Men

So, I spent my weeks in the healer's realm, the most relaxing of realms, home to the Dwarfs, animals, trees, and occasionally other healers, like fairies and Elves.

After spending time with the brilliant healers, I was reminded what wondrous storytellers they are, with many to tell since the beginning of time. One particular story caused a stir. It was once a vague memory, but now I fear history may be repeating itself, and their tale must be told.

It is my lifelong undertaking to deliver children's prayers and wishes to source—the puppeteer of the realms. I feel it is my duty to bring such stories to your attention. Without the human realm, your wishes can't be granted, and prayers won't be heard.

A tale of a mysterious landing on the human realm, gained the attention of two children named Beth and James—unlikely friends, forced together in hopes of solving a mystery. Some when in the year 2030, the Primagers are emerging and times are changing.

Chapter 1

Beth peeked behind the open curtains, dressed as a clown with her copper curly bunches, matching the fire buckets on stage. Her head rested in her palms as she viewed her older three brothers, Rod 14, Rowan 15 and Fin 17, perform the trio comedy and sword swallowing acts, which to this day still bore her.

Her mother and father ran away with the circus at 16 and 17, now they deliver a family show of

Pillars of Matchstick Men

acrobatics and archery for the world to see, since 1989.

On the other side of the curtain awaited a duo clown act, named the Diablo's. The towns' longstanding performance in the Giant Oak carnival. They were partners of the circus before Beth's parents joined. Draped in white, their main purpose was to outdo one another through silent actions of idiotic slips and trips. This was popular with the younger audience and an outlet for adults who wish they could act on their impulses without repercussions.

The drumroll, lights and the heat of the fire-jugglers wafted downstage. Beth's adrenaline rushed, it was soon her time to set the stage as the youngest fire-eater in the world, and the silliest clown in town at the tender age of 12.

The crowd clapped with the finale, a roar rippled across the outside theatre. A sound Beth knew came with disappointment. It was the moment in which her family stepped backstage with no words of encouragement for her.

After three years performing the same tricks, the pressure still builds daily, to do better.

Her palms were clammy, the thud of her heartbeat flooded her ears. She muttered to herself as she jumped up and down. "Just get on with it. You can do this... today is the day to show the world what you're made of."

Beth tightened her overall straps and adjusted her leather baton bolsters. She grabbed the fire batons from her backpack, twirled them in preparation. Her grip squeaked on the handles, white powder wafted in the air. Her dad spoke on the mic and announced, "And now, give a warm carnival welcome, to the fire breathing, daring Bethsational."

She stepped through the curtains with confidence and courage. A born performer, she thrived to make people laugh.

Her painted on smile, glowed as the spot light shone down. She dipped her batons in the fuel and lit them up, spinning them round, it was an incredible sight. Sparks flew, gasps from the

Pillars of Matchstick Men

audience filled her with confidence. Then for the finale she filled her mouth with fuel, a dangerous and deadly trick. Her father announced on the microphone, "Do not try this at home, laddettes and gentles, for what you are about to see has been practiced in controlled conditions."

Beth brought one of the fire batons up to her mouth and ate the fire. She spat out the fuel, and the sparks flew, she was a dragon of the night. The fiercest 12-year-old in Giant Oak.

Beth bowed before she left the stage, back behind the curtain.

"Phew, glad that's over, it's way too hot tonight," she said to her brother Rod. Darkness and whispers came as a relief. By the time she had walked off stage her family had waltzed back onto it.

"Well, thank you very much!" Beth said, as Rod walked away. "Three years performing for you and nothing. Well you can all break a leg!" She smeared her makeup leaving red and white streaks across her face.

Beth stormed out of the carnival ring to get some fresh air. Her private quiet spot was in the field nearby, which lay on the edge of a dark forest, the type that lured you in with its stillness.

A strange phenomenon appeared on the human realm, leaving four stone pillars known as the Enigma Pillars. The landing took place long before the Townsfolk arrived in Giant Oak.

The stones stood at 7ft tall, and occupied a boy named James, for which the pillars provided an eerie quiet place for the summer, where he could think for himself and not be interrupted by the locals. Beth and James regularly exchanged a few words and a nod here and there with minimal eye contact. Beth was certain he was from out of town and not from the surrounding areas.

The town's people were introverted and did not embrace newcomers well. The town's tales and fears had seeped into their ancestry beliefs and were clear today.

Pillars of Matchstick Men

A silent understanding between the townsfolk and outsiders were well known for years. But as times are changing, so are the myths and people.

Beth stormed toward the stones and spotted James sat behind one, wearing a bright orange raincoat, you couldn't miss him. Beth was not the regular 'town's people'. She had lived there for her entire life, but she was different, perhaps you'd say... slightly eccentric.

"Boo!" said Beth, with her smeared makeup in his face.

James gasped and rocked himself back and forth, with a fixed glare at the grass.

"Are you ok?" asked Beth, "What are you doing?" She stepped back and frowned with her hands on her hips, as she heard a mumbling.

James took a deep breath and counted slowly to 11.

"One Mississippi, two Mississippi..."
Beth whistled, to drown out his counting.

"Have you finished?" she asked.

"Yes… Please don't do that again … I … I'm not good with surprises, causes anxiety."

"What's that?"

"I'm not good with bangs or things that make me jump."

Beth rolled her eyes. "Better stay away from the carnival then." She smirked. "Why are you wearing a rain coat? It's a lovely day!"

James pondered for a moment. "Hmm, I suppose it's my favourite colour and I heard it rains a lot here."

Beth raised her eyebrows, knowing he was a newbie. "Yeh, I guess it does. But it's the end of summer, the sky is beautiful and I'm making the most of it!" Beth twirled around in her flared dungarees. "What are you doing today?" she asked.

"Um… not much, mum's working the market across the field, so I hang out here."

"Oh, tell me about it. My parents are on stage right now flying around the theatre."

A grin brightened his face. "That sounds fun."

Pillars of Matchstick Men

"I suppose for some. But, when you have been doing it for years, it gets boring. They hardly notice me any way."

Beth slid her back against the rock and wedged herself next to James.

"It's ok, I won't bite." Beth sniffed her armpit discreetly, wondering why he squirmed.

"Wanna go in there?" she pointed to the eerie woods straight in front.

"Not today thanks." James nibbled on his lower lip.

"Aww, are you afraid of the dark?"

James didn't respond.

"Ha, you are!"

He frowned. "Well I don't want to leave the field, my mum knows I'm here, so I shouldn't wander off."

"Mummy's boy I see."

"No, I am not! been separated from her before and don't want to go through that again." He stood up with his fists clenched by his sides.

"OK, OK, I understand, you got issues."

James stormed off toward the other rock, 10 paces to the right.

Beth was used to people walking away, but normally just her family, an odd feeling came over her.

Beth tailed him, and honked her bright red nose, followed by a goofy foot dance. She froze with a finale and waited for a response.

James did not even blink.

"Hello?" said Beth. "Oh, come on, that was funny." She huffed and pulled out her soft baton and accidently tripped over a stone on the floor and landed on her bottom, which caused a honking sound from a tiny horn placed in her back pocket— for stage effect.

James laughed, revealing a toothy smile with a large gap between his two front teeth.

"That's better. Come on now, let's play. I've only got an hour before I'm back on stage. You're welcome to watch me."

"No, that's ok, I've got my therapist this evening."

Pillars of Matchstick Men

Beth frowned with confusion. "I didn't think people actually did that. Is it fun?"

"Not really, I just talk about stuff, sometimes it can help."

Beth scratched her wig and nodded, she was trying very hard not to say anything rude.

"My therapist is nice, you'd like her, and she's kind and funny."

"Oh, I see..." Beth dug her oversized clown shoes into the dirt around the stone, kicking up mud. "Well this is fun," she said.

"Oh, you wanna see what I found today?" James adjusted his trousers and reached into his pocket, patched with a tartan square.

"Go on then, better be interesting."

"I found this stone by the fourth pillar."

Beth could not believe her eyes, "That's it? A stone?"

"Yes, but look, follow me."

Beth let out a growl sound and reluctantly followed James as he trudged his way toward the fourth pillar. Both hands in his pocket, shoulders up to his ears.

"Right here, this is where I found it." James pointed toward a hole in the rock pillar, about the size of his fist.

"It was just resting in the stone, like it was placed there. So, I poked it and it fell."

"Let me see," said Beth, she grabbed it and threw it across the field. James's face sunk.

He squeaked under his breath, "But I liked that rock."

"This is useless," said Beth as she began to walk away back to the carnival.

James kept his eyes locked firmly on the rocks path as it crash-landed onto the first pillar opposite.

A bright iridescent glow shone through the rock as it cracked on the ground. James power walked towards it. "Beth, Beth, come here look at this."

"What is it now?" She said. As she turned around noticing James walk faster.

"The rock, it's opened and ... glowing!"

Pillars of Matchstick Men

"Sounds like a carnival trick," said Beth.

James picked up the pieces, which split into two. He tried to line up the cracks and put it back together, the light still glowed through, he pulled it apart.

"Or maybe it's a gift from the Primagers?"

"Close it, close it," replied Beth covering her eyes. "You can't seriously believe in the Primagers? I've never seen one and the carnival is full of oddballs."

"Well you hear all these stories at school and in the news about the ancient witches and wizards now walking among us. Why can't it be real?"

Beth shook her head and grabbed the rock.

"What do you suppose it is?" she asked. "looks radioactive?"

James shook his head, "Not in these parts, this is something not from our world."

"Well, you keep getting weirder and weirder, but I like it!" said Beth.

"That's the nicest thing you've ever said to me."

James pulled the rock apart; he dropped it to the floor as the brightness blinded him.

"Look, there's something inside it," said Beth.

James knelt to see, it was a tiny piece of paper, rolled up into a scroll. He struggled to read the water damaged words, leaving only pictures to decipher.

Chapter 2

James pressed the car door shut as he yelled, "I'll see you in an hour, Mum."

He stood in front of a tall stone building and counted 35 steps on every visit.

He gripped the golden handles on the outside and took a deep breath in, he muttered, "It's only an hour, I can do this."

As James walked from the entrance to Dr. Sturgeon's office, the hallway seemed to never end.

The smell of freshly baked biscuits wafted through the door. The most welcoming scent possible.

Dr Sturgeon sat in her green leather, high—back armchair. Hovering above her right hand spun three Chinese glass balls. The other arm was locked in a solid cast, her finger moved clockwise above her mug, stirring her beverage. These were tricks of a Primis Mage or the Primagers, Ones born of the human realm yet strung together with magic DNA, you may know them as wizards and witches. Humans have been stripped of all powers today, yet some still linger within their blood, these are the Primagers.

The wallpaper was designed with cats staring in every direction.

She scurried across the room, leaving the balls hovering. With a waft of her hand the files on the desk were organised, stacked and neatly pressed against the wall.

"Today is the day, I will rid those pesky lurchers once and for all. I'll not have them interfere with my client's therapy, any more," said Dr. Sturgeon.

Pillars of Matchstick Men

The cleansing biscuits, mixed with a lurcher detox potion, flew from the back-office oven into a wicker bowl at the meeting table. An elixir prescribed for those humans with an unfortunate pest, known as lurchers—a shadow that feeds on fear and negativity. Pests are loyal to their masters yet drain their victims' energy.

The clock spun as the time fast forward to the correct hour of 4.45pm. Time can't be stopped within the human realm, but some had mastered the art of time manipulation.

James stood in front of the large wooden door titled 'Dr Sturgeons' Office'. He took one final deep breath in for courage. As he reached the bronzed doorknob, a soft voice blew through the door.

"Is that you James?" said Dr. Sturgeon.

"How does she know? Every time... Yes, it's me," he said, opening the door.

"Well come on in, there's a nice plate of biscuits waiting for you, my secretary brought them in from her daughter's school." She wiped the crumbs from her bright purple lips. "That should clear the cobwebs, or should I say lurchers."

"Lurchers?" asked James.

"What dear? Oh, you know, cobwebs... just a bit of sugar to pep you up." She passed him a biscuit. "Take a seat. How are you this evening?"

"I'm ok, thanks... Oh, what happened to your arm?" James noticed she had her left arm in a cast.

"I fell off a ladder at home whilst watering my plants. Unlike me, I usually have a steady step. So, my secretary bought in the biscuits. As a get well soon gesture."

"Oh, I see."

"Enough about me, how are you?"

"Moving forward, I guess."

"Indeed, this is our 12th session now. I will jump straight into it, Ok?"

Before James responded, Dr Sturgeon had her pen to her paper, sat upright in the throne-like arm chair.

"So, how are the nightmares? What was your most recent one?"

Pillars of Matchstick Men

James took a deep breath and tapped his fingers on his knees; he paused for a moment and looked up to ceiling to gather his thoughts.

"You won't find the answers up there, dear boy. Was it that bad?"

"Well, it was just last night."

"Mm, I see, go on."

"It's more of a knowing really, than it actually happening, if that makes sense?"

Dr Sturgeon rested her glasses on the tip of her nose and nodded, staring at him.

"Well, the world gets taken over by this eerie darkness, I don't know where it comes from. It's in an instant, and then... the fear takes over. It's like a portal opens for all the bad things to come in."

"And what do you think that means?"

"I'm afraid of the world ending?"

"Or you feel helpless? Perhaps it's time to put action in and make a difference. Maybe a good deed, or helping the needy, so you see the world is good?"

"I suppose I could try that."

"Have you had the dream before?" she asked.

"No, this was the first time."

"Ok, well I'll take a note and well see if it ever reoccurs. Remember that dreams are just a way of our minds giving us the tools to process our fears and release any worries. It is as though our subconscious is preparing us for the worst, which in effect enables us to cope better if situations were to arise," said Dr Sturgeon. "Obviously your dream is different and reflects your inner fears, which enables you to talk about them in your waking life which allows for healing."

James sat there with bewilderment; he never saw it that way. She paused for a moment and allowed it to sink in.

"How is the counting coming along?"

"Most times I can count to 21 and then my thoughts calm down, and I can get back to sleep."

"And how about during the day?"

"Since I've moved things have been better, but I've met this girl and she's a bit loud, fun but crazy and every time she makes me jump, I have to count

Pillars of Matchstick Men

to 9, but then I'm ok." James tapped his fingers together to calm himself. "She breathes fire at the carnival."

Dr. Sturgeon completely changed her stance, sitting up in her chair with a hopeful smile on her face.

"Well that sounds new and interesting. Sometimes people opposite to us are usually just what we need in a friend, I'm happy for you."

"Her family is bizarre, I thought mine were strange."

"Oh, I've seen some strange things in this room and trust me families are at the top."

The hour ticked by in a matter of a fairy flutter. James left the Doctor's office feeling optimistic, first time in a while. He straightened up his shirt and walked with a boost in his stride. James opened the front doors with all his might and stepped onto the top concrete step, sniffing the fresh air with a sigh of relief.

As he skipped down the stairs, his mother's red camper van awaited him, stocked with metal bars and bright flowing clothes for the market.

"How was that sweetheart?"

"It went well, are you still working this evening?" asked James.

"Yes, It's the harvest market, goes 'til late. But you are welcome to play in the field again or go visit the carnival."

James rolled his eyes, there was only so much fun a field could offer.

"Let's grab a quick bite at the market?" she asked.

James grinned and rested his head on her shoulder as she drove back to town.

The autumn sun set across the rolling hills. This was James's favourite time of the year. The bright colours reminded him that life can be fun.

The suns glow perfectly beamed across the carnival stage, Beth had lit the way with her fire breathing and spinning skills.

Pillars of Matchstick Men

With no plans and a lot of time on his hands, James decided he would visit the carnival to spot Beth, but he daren't show his face. He crept around the back of the stage, a large trailer with five doors. One was wide open with a wooden star plaque, hanging on a string. The corridor littered with resting bodies.

As he stepped carefully across the sleeping performers, he heard a scuffle and odd sounds from behind a mesh curtain. He knew he was not supposed to be back stage. Reaching for the veil that parted them, he peaked behind and saw two clowns dressed in white clothes and simple white painted faces.

"Well they're odd looking, pretty boring actually." He whispered. They repeatedly hit each other with batons, in an uncontrollable manor.

"What are they doing?" he said.

Each clown did not seem to react; it was as though they were puppets or robots.

"This place gets weirder and weirder," James muttered.

The clowns suddenly noticed they were being watched. They frowned at James and pointed at him through the darkness.

"Oh no," said James as he walked backwards away from the carnival. Carefully stepping back over the sleeping performers. The clowns did not move, they stared at him the entire way.

"I think I've had enough for one day," said James, he rushed away, eager not to look back. On the outskirts of the carnival was an information board. An illustration of the first circus shows in 1768. James stopped to read it.

"Well at least they don't use animals any more. But the people are freaky."

He clambered over the hill toward the Enigma pillars.

He sat in his resting place where he once felt calm and relaxed, but now with Beth's habit to jump up at him, he became restless.

The sun now set, a breeze blew through the woods across the field, leaving an eerie feeling as the darkness oozed from the trees into the field.

Pillars of Matchstick Men

He sat behind the pillar where he found the small stone and rocked back and forth counting to calm his nerves. Since his recent nightmare, the dark has become something even more to fear. He gasped as he clocked a rustling and movement in the trees. Was it his imagination or creatures of the night?

"It's not real, it's not real. Nothing can hurt me," said James, trying to self soothe.

He couldn't help himself but look toward the woods, squinting hoping to distort his view. James felt something was watching him.

The sound of rustling and chiming bells rang closer.

Chapter 3

A high-pitched horn noise pierced James's ear as Beth slumped to the ground next to him.

"I've finished my shows for the night, just the adults doing their stuff now, want to play?"

James stared at her hyperventilating through his nose, "I told you not to do that again!"

Pillars of Matchstick Men

Beth rolled her eyes and said, "It's getting late, why are you still here?"

James tried to catch his breath, "Mum's... at the harvest market for a little longer."

"OH, no dad?"

"No, he died when I was a baby."

Beth nodded and said, "Oh, I'm sorry. At least you won't have him yell at you for doing the wrong things."

"I don't know, your dad probably just wants to make sure you're safe."

Beth laughed, "Yeh right! Well, at least you're happy."

James frowned, "What could you be unhappy about? You live with the carnival."

Beth twiddled her batons and whistled to distract him.

"Have you still got the stupid scroll and rock?"

James paused and checked his pocket, "Oh yep, here it is. I forgot about that." The bright bluey glow lit an aura of light around them.

"I wonder what these pictures mean." James squinted and brought the paper up to his nose. "It looks as though it's been stitched. Could be a leaf... I'm not sure, you look."

"Give it 'ere, my vision is pinpoint perfect."

James passed the scroll to Beth.

"Yeh, it's a leaf and an arrow pointing to a hole in the dirt. What do you think that means?"

"I'm not sure, this place gives me the creeps."

"Wanna hear a creepy story?" asked Beth.

"Maybe..." he said, reluctantly.

"See the wood over there." Beth pointed to the edge of the field where a dark wall of trees loomed. "Well... it's called Giant Oak, but did you know it's hexed, guarded by giants, but obviously never seen. No one ever goes in there unless they have a screw loose or a death wish. If anyone has gone in, they never come out again." Beth rubbed her hands together as though she was concocting a plan.

"Giant Oak is full of gossips and oldies. Dunno if you've noticed. Story has it the woods is a portal

Pillars of Matchstick Men

to another world or parallel universe. Wouldn't it be amazing to find the portal and just vanish?"

James' eyebrows raised with wonder.

"A few children have gone missing in the past ten years. It's said that as soon as you step one foot across the grass you would never return." Beth stood a head taller than James as she wiggled her fingers in his face to spook him.

"Sounds like a lovely story, or nightmare." James didn't believe in this sort of thing.

"Wanna test it out?"

"No, I'm ok thanks, I've already heard strange sounds from those woods, I'll just wait here until my mum comes and gets me."

"Look, there's something over there." Beth pointed to the wood. "Did you hear that?"

"Ha-ha, very funny. It's probably just a deer or something."

"That doesn't look like a deer... it's got two legs and is walking this way," said Beth.

James stood up and reluctantly peered behind the pillar. Through the darkness, he saw the outline of a person in a top hat drawing near.

"It's a Primager!" James squeaked.

"Don't be ridiculous!" Beth stood with her hands on her hips and kept her eyes locked on the figure. James still behind the pillar, peeked through his fingers.

As the figure crept closer, Beth honked her horn, to see its reaction.

"Oh, it's just a performer from the carnival, I expect he went for a walk."

James frowned at Beth. "Never come back, hey?"

"Well, I said it was just a story."

"He looks different from the guys you work with."

"How do you know who I work with?"

James blushed. "I explored backstage and saw your crew, some were asleep and there were a few more, odd clowns. But they were not wearing a top

Pillars of Matchstick Men

hat or as well dressed as him or... with water dripping from their ankles."

"You're right... water?" asked Beth.

The man dressed as smart as they come, penguin suit and a dusty, black bowler hat. He kicked his ankles to shake the water away.

Beth and James took a few steps back as the figure edged closer. He took off his top hat and bowed to them, smartened his suit and twisted his back as it cracked. He let out a groan of relief.

"It's not what you think, honestly," said the stranger, ringing out his trouser pockets.

Beth sneered, "Why are you so wet?"

"It's my... super power, or curse, it was an embarrassment growing up. I'm sure you could imagine."

James nodded.

"Oh, it's been a while since I've moved, it's so nice to get out of there."

"Where did you come from?" asked Beth.

"I've been trapped in between for some time. So, I assume it is your doing that set me free? Thank you eternally." The stranger bowed to them.

Beth looked and James with a raised lip. "You've got the wrong idea, we haven't done anything to help you. Just hanging out by the pillars," said Beth.

"I've been warned about talking to strangers, I'm not sure," said James. "My mum will be here any minute."

"Oh lovely," said the stranger.

"Who are you?" asked James.

The crooked man tucked his hand up his sleeve and pulled out a cane.

"I'm Veranga, from the realm of healers, not far from here. But I have been between for some time." Veranga walked around the pillars, stroking each one. "It's been too long, my friends," he said.

"Who are you talking to?" asked Beth.

"My friends. What year is this, dear?"

"It's 2030, all year!"

Pillars of Matchstick Men

Veranga raised his top hat and shook it at the sky as though telling someone off.

"It's been far too long, I need your help. I take it you found the scroll?" asked Veranga.

"How do you know about that?" asked Beth.

"Well children, finding that, has been my release. We do not have long." Veranga slammed his cane into the ground and chanted. "Twelve hours from the rise of the forest the woodland and the pillars. We will awake when the elements are settled, four pillars of the wind, fire, earth and water. So, let it be."

Beth sniggered.

Veranga twitched his bushy grey moustache and pointed his finger into the air. "Have you solved the riddle yet?" Veranga asked.

"You mean the pictures?"

"Yes." Veranga rolled up his sleeves, eager for an answer.

"Well, it looks like an oak leaf with an arrow pointing to a hole in the ground?

"Correct, what do you suppose that means?" asked Veranga.

"Do we have to bury an oak leaf?" asked James.

"What good would that do?" Beth was confused. "I don't understand, it's getting late and I have a lot of work tomorrow."

"Time is not on our side, dear girl. You cannot leave now." In that second, Veranga shook his sleeve and pulled out a large scroll which read:

Those who greet you from the woods are the ones who must complete the three tasks to set the realms again. Time will stand still for no one.

A reset must be completed.

The time will come and now it must be, the watches are to be given and set in sync. Gifts to realm must be given, to release what couldn't be done at the beginning.

Pillars of Matchstick Men

The scroll rolled back and slipped up his sleeve, he took his hat off and in each hand appeared two iridescent blue wrist watches.

"These are for you, I have set them exactly as they should be. Do not muddle with time. Great danger will arise if these are left in the wrong hands. And remember you have twelve hours to complete the tasks, or all will be lost again."

"What tasks? You expect us to stay awake for 12 hours!"

"Oh, come on Beth, it's an adventure," said James. He paused for a moment. "I can't believe I'm saying this, but I need excitement in my life."

Beth gasped. "You want to do this? We don't even know what we're doing!"

"That's the best part, oh come on, we can figure this out, its 12 hours, not a lifetime."

"Well unfortunately your time is now ten and a half hours," said Veranga. "The time started ticking when you released me from my pillar. The moment you cracked the scroll, your time began again."

"Oh, even better then," said Beth as she shook her head, feeling defeated.

Veranga clapped three times, the sounds echoed across the field. He pointed to the stars in a clear night sky and waved his hands in fluid motion, 4 stars shone the brightest above them.

"Wow," said Beth, "I've never seen the sky so clear before."

"I'm no astrologer, but those stars aren't meant to be there, are they?" asked James.

"You're right my lad, but tonight is the night, these are the four pillars which must be unlocked to reset."

"Reset?" asked James.

"Everything'll be ok. As long as we complete the reset. Just like the bears in winter and the seasons that follow, resets are a crucial part of life to thrive and survive. Without it, your world will not be so strong. The universe wants you to complete these tasks, which only a human can do."

Beth snarled, "What a load of twaddle," she said. "There are 6 bright stars up there."

Pillars of Matchstick Men

Veranga adjusted his hat and pulled out a pair of round glasses to inspect.

He grunted and said, "Yes, well let's ignore those two and focus on the other four. Each star represents the four pillars here. See the brightest?" Veranga pointed to the sky. "That represents me, I am free. When you release each pillar, its star will glow. We are all connected and so are you."

"I think it's fun," said James.

"You realise, it's night time and would be doing this in the dark?" said Beth.

James sighed, "I thought you weren't afraid of anything?"

Beth locked her folded arms tightly to her chest and pursed her lips to stop any further remarks from slipping.

Veranga coughed to gain their attention. "Now, now..." He rustled up his sleeves again and splashed golden dust through the air, the dust moved smoothly across the sky above them forming a bioluminescent blob.

A.K. Baxter

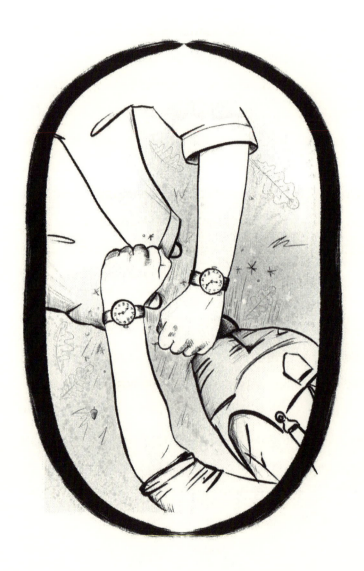

Pillars of Matchstick Men

"Say hello to your Luminarium, these are your very own local glow worms. Still young and will need to be taken care of, no dropping them or shaking them. You understand?"

Beth and James stood in awe, gazing up at the sky nodding.

Veranga held out his hands and a jar appeared in each. "One for you, James, and one for you Beth." With a swish of his hands the glowing blobs parted and entered each jar. "Quick the lids," said Veranga, he clicked his fingers and the jars hung from their necks on a rope. "These will light your way into the darkness, but if they feel threatened their light will go out and since there is only about another 10 hours of darkness, I'd hurry. I must stay here by these pillars. Stay on the right path and you will find your way."

With their wrist watches set to exactly 7:42 pm, time started to tick.

Chapter 4

Beth rubbed her eyes and yawned, stretching her arms to the sky and said, "I don't really understand what we're doing, why don't we go home?"

"And pass up this adventure? I thought you were fun."

Pillars of Matchstick Men

"Some of us have worked all day." Beth huffed and rolled her eyes.

James murmured in agreement. "That's fair, but come on, who was the last person to walk out of those woods? I believe we're in the right place at the right time."

Beth rested her hands on her hips and mimicked James's actions.

"Ok, that's fine, I'll work out this scroll on my own." He opened it one more time to double check what it was. "Perhaps we need to find an Oak tree?"

"You mean those over there?" Beth pointed to the dark forest ahead.

"I believe they are Willow trees?" said James.

"Yeah, but beyond those are Giant Oaks. You think we need to go in there?" asked Beth.

James paused for a moment and cringed. "Unfortunately, I think we do. Maybe it's time to test out your stories."

Beth grinned, eager to finally take the steps across the border. "All right then, I guess were really doing this. Parallel universe here I come!"

"No, you can't leave now or visit some other universe. We need to complete these tasks. Didn't you hear Veranga?"

Beth sighed and tightened her batons to her back.

"Yeah, I did. Don't blame me if we don't come back."

James bit his lip. "Maybe I should leave a note for Mum?"

Beth laughed and said, "Why not light a flare whilst you're at it."

James took a deep breath, the biggest he had taken all day.

"As long as were in and then out!" James held on tightly to his glow worms around his neck.

"Agreed," said Beth as she crossed her fingers behind her back.

The sound of crunching autumn leaves led the way across the field to the grassy edge of the wood. The trees stood glooming over them like the caves of the Intrepidus Gorge.

Beth nudged his arm and said, "Well we're this far, may as well go in." After 12 years of her life living in that town, she had never stood that close to the wood. James looked up to the sky one last time to check the four stars were still above.

"Ready? We'll go together, one, two, and three," said Beth. On three she pushed James into the forest.

"What d'ya do that for?" James frowned as Beth laughed. Her smeared, painted on smile made for eerie company.

She caught her breath and said, "I... I couldn't help myself. I'm coming." Beth leapt over the grass into the wood with all her might.

The darkness took over, no lights above to guide them.

"Surely, we don't need to go far in. But what are we looking for?" James gasped as he stood under a Giant Oak and looked up. "These are massive!" He placed his hands on the tree feeling the rough bark. A gust of wind blew into the wood, creaks and moans echoed.

"I don't think were alone in here," he said.

"It's only the woods, silly. Maybe we'll find the portal to another dimension, and I can get out'a here once and for all!"

"I quite like our world, you don't know how good you've got it," said James.

Spread across the forest bed were tree roots mangled and large which made for a great obstacle course. They trod carefully, weaving through the roots and branches.

"I don't like this," said James, his breath becoming shallow.

"Just follow me," said Beth.

James looked up through the canopy to see the moon aglow; the stars were no longer visible. Holes where old oaks trees once stood now left craters in the ground. James held his glow worms up above his head to help navigate his way through the roots.

"Watch out for these holes, Beth. I don't think we should go much further in."

There was no response. Only the sound of owls and crows squawking, trees moaning and roots

Pillars of Matchstick Men

creaking. James looked back to the forest edge eager to run back.

"BETH, where are you?"

A scream came from the distance, and with that so did the trees awakening.

James scurried toward the scream hoping to find Beth. The roots squirmed, and the trees swayed, stretching their branches behind him as though trying to grab him.

He called out to Beth yet again. This time came no answer. A tiny glow gained his attention. Buried beneath the roots within a crater were shining glow worms.

Beth laid there with her finger to her lips, shushing James. She daren't move. He reached into the crater and grabbed her arm.

A.K. Baxter

Pillars of Matchstick Men

"Do not move, they will catch you too," she whispered. "I'm not ready to die, I don't really want to go to another dimension."

A minute went by, in silence. "What do we do?" asked James.

"They are calming down, we wait until they sleep," said Beth. James buried his head into his coat in disbelief.

The trees were silent, the roots were still, nothing moved in that forest. After a few minutes of silence, Beth said, "Psst, pull me out quietly."

"Oh finally, that felt like forever!"

James on his belly grabbed both of her arms and pulled as hard as he could, leaving both covered in mud. The moment she was free, she let out a cry of relief. The trees awoke, grinding and flailing as though they were hungry. They ran as fast as they could to the forests edge. Leaves and branches were flung across the wood, acorns used as bullets shot at their heads.

"Ouch!" yelled Beth. Acorns struck her Jar of glow worms. "My glow worms aren't as glowy anymore."

"Just keep going," said James. "Stay close to me." James grabbed Beth's hand. "Wait... that's it! The acorns! try to collect some, quick."

"There's no time for this." Beth yelled as she kept on running.

James scampered across the ground and collected as many as he could, making his way out of the forest.

With his pocket full of acorns they both fell to the ground the moment they touched the grass.

"What the heck was that about?" asked Beth.

"Your story is true."

They both stepped back in awe of their escape, the trees still moaned and loud cracks and whips of their branches echoed across the field.

"These are what we needed to find!" James emptied his pockets and knew what he had to do.

"Acorns, why?"

Pillars of Matchstick Men

"My mum used to call them fairy goblets, we can bury it and it will grow into an oak tree."

Beth looked at the scroll and said, "Will that work?"

"It's worth a try." James ran all the way back to pillars, "We made it!"

"Yes, good for us," she said in a monotone voice, trying to hide her relief.

James got on his hands and knees dug a hole by the side of the first pillar where he found the scroll. He looked at Beth and said, "Come and help me dig."

"Will this grow into an oak tree?" asked James.

Beth shrugged her shoulders.

He patted down the earth and laid grass and leaves on top. He stood up and stepped back to admire his work.

"Ah, now what I wonder?"

"Off to bed for me," said Beth as she walked away toward her trailer at the carnival.

"You can't go, we've only got a few more hours to do this. And my mum hasn't shown up yet. Please stay."

"You mean more hours! That's a long time to hang around for nothing."

"You obviously believe in something or wouldn't have hung around when the man walked out of the woods, unharmed," said James. "That's a point...where did Veranga go?"

Beth chuckled to herself. "See, even the mystery man can't stand around for nothing."

"Maybe he's invisible?"

"Yeah, alright then," said Beth as she patted James on the back.

Beth sat down rested against the pillar, she knew it would only be a matter of time before James wanted to go home too.

"Well, James...what now?"

"Wait, I guess. I wonder where my mum has got to."

"Perhaps she forgot about you and is all tucked up in bed."

Pillars of Matchstick Men

James frowned and elbowed her. "My mum's not like that, she would never forget me."

"Well mine are currently flying across the stage performing an 'I love you' act, makes me want to puke, every time they swing to each other I secretly wish one of them to fall."

James's jaw dropped with disbelief. "How can you say that?"

"Oh, I don't really, but sometimes..."
The lights were visible from the pillars and the sounds of the audience cheers rippled across the field.

"Ah, hello, glad you completed the scroll," said Veranga, making his way toward the buried acorn.

James and Beth leapt up when they heard his voice appear from nowhere. "Where the heck did you come from?" asked Beth.

"I've always been here."

James looked at Beth and said, "See."

"Unless I wasn't here at all and have confused today with last time?" Veranga scratched his head and shook his top hat. "Hmm, maybe that will help; I seem to be foggy still."

Beth slapped her palm into her face.

"Any who," said Veranga, he placed his hands above the acorn and closed his eyes. An instant golden light spewed from his hands into the earth.

"Look!" said James. "He's making it grow!"

The acorn sprouted through the earth and out popped a stem and leaves. "It doesn't seem to be stopping," said Beth. "How?"

Veranga opened his eyes and simply said, "We healers can speed up growth and help life spark where ever."

Beth huffed and said, "Oh give me a break."

The plant stood about two metres tall, strong, with plenty of life and room to grow.

"Did you not just see that with your eyes?" asked James.

"Of course, I did, but he's a trickster, for all I know he's a rival of our carnival."

"Ok, Beth. Whatever you want to believe."

Pillars of Matchstick Men

As Veranga moved his hands away from the growing acorn, he opened his palms revealing another bright blue light. James moved in for a closer look.

"Wow, what is that?" he asked.

"You've unlocked a scroll, take it, it's yours. But remember time is still ticking and with every scroll requires a riddle to be answered. Go with haste and a clear head on your shoulders."

Veranga passed the scroll to James and said, "My job is done, I cannot help my friends any more. It's up to you two now. Thank you."

James and Beth looked at one another in confusion.

"That's it? Now you're leaving?" asked Beth. As they looked ahead, Veranga had disappeared yet again.

Beth shook her head in disbelief, "Now that's a super power I could use occasionally."

James nodded in agreement.

Chapter 5

Beth grabbed the scroll, an eye of a bird glowed a blue aura on one side and on the other was a piece of ancient writing, which read:

From gods of old and new, nurturing food and transformations, bring forth the earthworms that feast upon your dirt. For some it is golden.

"Oh, I hate riddles," said Beth.

Pillars of Matchstick Men

"Well it's a good thing I enjoy them," said James.

"Earthworms?" said Beth, "This keeps getting better."

"Why do you take things so literally, perhaps it means something else?"

"Go on then, do tell."

James crossed his arms and closed his eyes, he tried to think what it could mean.

The minutes were ticking, the stars were bright as the darkness thickened on the ground. There was still no sign of James's mother. It was as though time elsewhere had stood still, and it was the children's time now.

"I suppose we could go home for a little and rest, I'm getting tired," said James.

"Ha, now you want to go, I thought you enjoyed riddles."

"I do, I just don't know where my mother is."

"Probably at the pub?"

"She doesn't drink, she would never leave me here, something isn't right."

In that moment Veranga coughed to gain their attention. "You can't leave now. You have less than eight hours to complete the tasks."

"Where the heck did you come from?" asked Beth.

James short of breath said, "You can't keep doing that. Have you not heard of knocking?"
Beth tutted at James and said, "What if I say no and go home right now?" asked Beth.

"Then your world will surely have no hope."

"That's a bit dramatic," said James, as he checked his watch, it read exactly 11:50pm.

Veranga waved his hand through the air, clearing the skies, he whispered, "Watch this."

A wispy cloud film played in front of them as the clouds swayed and formed images upon the skyline. An image of their world today, the globe and the animals running away, to their extinction. The trees clear-cut and the melting glaciers, slipping off the face of the earth. Man fighting man and stealing, war and anger flooded the streets. Veranga made a sad face and drew a tear on his

Pillars of Matchstick Men

face, he cleared the skies and revealed the timeline since humans began and the damage that had been caused. Over the course of the worlds' existence there has been numerous resets but none with success since the dawn of man.

"Your world hangs on by mere threads, it is only a matter of time before your world wreaks havoc as the darkness takes over. No more answered prayers or wishes. No more connection to source, you will be truly alone."

A large red button appeared before them, labelled 'RESET'.

Beth and James stood silent, their mouths open wide, hypnotised by the wispy chaos.

"Now, don't you think your world needs a reset?"

"What do you mean?" asked James.

"Have you ever wondered about those moments of déjà vu? Or why the seasons are so erratic? These are voices of your intuition, source and guides yelling at you to make a change, warning you about your situation. Complete these tasks and you shall awaken the four pillars, the original chosen ones to reset your world. But they failed and have been locked away since."

Beth laughed with hysteria, but then stopped abruptly and sighed, "You're having me on?"

Veranga walked past the four pillars and stroked each of them until he got back to the first pillar. He pushed his hand into the centre and watched it disintegrate into dust.

"I'am free because of you, my friends are still stuck. You must take the responsibility of your actions, no one else can complete them for you. You must finish what you started." Veranga disappeared.

"Come on now Beth, time is a ticking," James kicked his toes out in a sort of jig. With a grin across his face, he tapped his watch.

"Yes, yes... I suppose so, I didn't have you down as an adventurer."

"Nor did I! But I'm a tad excited, aren't you?"

A smile cracked from her lips.

Pillars of Matchstick Men

"Right, these worms... well mine don't seem to up to much. Why don't we offer my worms to the pillar?" Beth stood in darkness, nothing but a light glow around her neck.

"Why would a pillar need worms? This seems very odd."

"Maybe it's not for the pillars and for the earth? I don't know but we should get on with it," said James.

Beth huffed and walked towards the second pillar. As she knelt to the ground she said, "Here will do?"

James shrugged his shoulders, "Your guess is as good as mine."

"Here pass me your glow worms so I can see 'ere."

James hesitated, "Be gentle ok, I happen to like my worms."

Beth snatched the jar from James's neck and shone the light at the bottom of the pillar.

"This'll have to do," she said as she dug a hole into the surrounding dirt.

Beth jolted the jar several times to release the worms, the earth lit up for a few seconds, until they all wriggled their way into the dirt.

Beth stood back and dusted off her hands. "Right, that outa do it."

They waited for a moment, James with his fingers crossed behind his back and Beth held up the last of the glow worms.

James murmured, "Um... I don't think that worked."

"Shh," said Beth, "just wait."

They waited... James clock watched every second.

"Ahem... it's been 3 minutes and 28 seconds... It didn't work!" he said.

"What a bloody waste of time that was, I knew this was a load of rubbish."

James tapped his head, there had to be another answer, "Come on... think, think," he said.

He paced around the pillar, tapping his fingers against each other as he walked.

"James, you're making me dizzy, now stop!"

Pillars of Matchstick Men

"You got any brighter ideas?" asked James.

Beth was about to say something in return, you could tell it wouldn't be very nice. But she stopped herself. Beth rubbed her forehead as though she was trying to squeeze out the answer.

"Aha, I know where we can get different worms."

"Worms again. Are you sure?"

"Have you got any better ideas?" asked Beth.

"Well no, actually."

"Right follow me." Beth power walked away from the pillars, over the hill and back to the carnival. The lights were off, no music to be heard.

"Don't tell me you're giving up already?" he asked.

"No, not any more. I'm here for the long haul. Beats being stuck in the trailer with all my brothers."

James let out a sigh of relief.

"Right, this path by the south entrance is used the most, and I remember on days where we were sold out, the worms would come to the surface from the trodden in disturbed mud."

"Oh ... but it hasn't rained in a while?"

"Perhaps not where you live, but it rains here every day. We have a sprinkler system for after the show which makes sure all the fire and equipment is safely put out."

Beth got on her hands and knees and sifted through the mud.

"Erm... Beth, I don't want to alarm you, but there are two men staring at us from your stage."

Beth instantly whispered, "Get down." She grabbed his shirt and pulled him behind the stands.

"They were the guys I was talking about earlier."

"They can't know I'm out of bed, they will tell mother." Beth squirmed. "They're weird like that. I don't even know why they are with us, but they have been for ... well since before I was born."

"And they've never left?"

"Nope, they've been here for as long as I can remember."

Pillars of Matchstick Men

"Do you think they saw you?"

"Oh yes," said James.

Beth growled. "What about me?"

He nodded yes, but said, "No, not at all..."

"Well I guess we will find out. Here, hold my jar."

Beth picked up the worms one by one and wiggled them in James face as she pretended to eat them.

"Yep, this town is definitely weird." James sneered.

"Ha, I'm not as weird as everyone else."

"Sure... as you pretend to eat worms and live with freaks, your words not mine."

"HEY, those freaks are my family and only I can call them that."

"Fair enough," said James as he tightened the lid on the jar.

"Ok, let's go back to the pillars now, it's 12:50."

"Just wait here for one moment, I'll be right back."

James tried to call out to her, but she had already run back to her trailer, on the north side of the carnival.

An eerie feeling set in, James twitched.

"Oh, come on Beth, there's something weird going on here."

A loud caw pierced James's ear. A large pigeon sat on the overhanging branch above him.

"Oh, hello bird," said James, trying to ease his nerves. "Lovely evening isn't it?"

The bird watched him, its white eyes studying his movements.

"You are quite the plump little bird, aren't you? Good place for leftover popcorn I'd imagine."

James nervously laughed at himself as he waited for Beth to come back.

The sound of squelching boots drew near. James peeked with one eye around the stands to check for Beth.

"Phew, thank god it's you."

"Aww, were you scared?" before James could answer, she showed him her backpack.

Pillars of Matchstick Men

"Look, I've got supplies." She pulled out some crisps, a bottle of water and some beads on a string.

"These are for luck, my grandmother made them." She took out a tin opener. "Oh, don't mind this, this was here from my last camp out."

Then she grabbed her torch.

"Ah, now this is useful, anything else handy in there?" asked James.

Beth flinched as she heard the pigeon above ruffle its feathers.

"Come on, let's go," she said.

Beth and James ran the whole way back to the pillars. "Quick behind the pillar," said Beth

"What is it?" asked James.

"Just making sure we're not being followed."

"What by the bird?" James chuckled.

"Well, you never know. But no, I meant the clowns, Merlot and Trent, or the Diablo's."

"You're sounding a little paranoid, this is why people need their sleep."

"You don't get it. My family are freaks, but these people... well they are actual weirdo's, like something isn't right about them."

"OK, it's alright, I don't think they saw you at all."

James took the worms from Beth's neck and gave her a gentle look, "let's do this, together."

Beth nodded. They tipped the jar upside down into the hole already dug.

"Fingers crossed," said James.

They both stood back with their arms linked and fingers crossed.

James could not help but check his watch every other second.

The long hand ticked away as he counted "5... 7... 9... 11." The pillar below rumbled, the earth crumbled below their feet.

James pulled Beth away from the pillar. "It worked!" he beamed at Beth and she smiled back as the earth rocked beneath them.

Chapter 6

The pillar crumbled away, leaving a dusty debris revealing a divine white owl, with piercing blue eyes which lit up the darkness.

The owl ruffled its feathers, twisting and jerking its neck.

"What is it doing?" asked James, rather confused.

"I don't know, but I would imagine being stuck in a rock for years would make you feel a little bit... stiff?"

James grumbled in agreement.

The owl spread out its wings, which reached over two metres across.

"Now what?" said Beth in frustration.

The bird stomped on the earth where the pillar once stood, it clawed deep into the soil and pulled out a worm with its beak, it gulped down the worms with a little effort one by one.

"Hungry I suppose?" said James.

The owl winked at him and carried on eating.

"Did you see that?" asked James, astonished.

"It was probably a blink." Beth rubbed her eyes to check she was still awake.

As it swallowed the final worm, a gratuitous burp seeped from its beak. It wiped its mouth with its wing and said, "Oh thank you so much dear ones. Let me introduce myself..."

James counted and rock back and forth. His breath became faster.

Pillars of Matchstick Men

"It's ok just relax," said Beth as she patted his back. "Look up at the stars, the second one is glowing. We did it!"

James smiled and wiped his eyes.

"You can talk?" he asked.

"My folks would love to have you as part of our act," added Beth.

"I'm afraid I can't do that for you. You see I am Athena, daughter of Zeus and goddess of counsel, wisdom and defence. I am here with a purpose."

James gathered his thoughts and worry turned into excitement.

"Goddess Athena, you say?"

The owl shimmered and bowed with a nod. "Call me Ethel."

He smirked at the thought. "I have been researching about the gods and have always enjoyed learning about them. But aren't you a..."

"Goddess?"

"I was going to say a lady... yes?"

In that moment Athena spun its neck around and stretched taller than the trees, as a whirlwind of feathers floated to the ground revealing a beautiful, fair- skinned lady, hair as gold as hay and eyes piercing blue.

Beth stood back in anticipation. She had not expected such a transformation from a worm-eating, nocturnal beast into a radiant goddess.

"Ok, this is good and all, but what are we supposed to do with you? You've torn up the ground and someone is bound to notice this malting mess you've left," said Beth.

Athena didn't know how to respond, other than cleaning up after herself. She tied her hair up in a top knot, her neck twisted just like the owl. As her body and flowing gown span round, the debris vanished.

"Ha, weird... but useful," said James, "I don't remember reading about that."

Beth in bewilderment, was quite entertained.

"My folks will really love her, I'd be out of a job for sure, or maybe my sister could finally move out." James elbowed Beth and shushed her as he put his finger to his lips.

Pillars of Matchstick Men

"Children of today, have you come across any other creatures of late?" asked Athena.

"If you mean Veranga, then yes... you could say we have." Beth snarled.

James butted in, "We've been told what you are here for and that you've tried to save our world before, but we don't really understand what we can do to help? Except wake you lot up."

Athena swished the back of her hand under James's chin, with a gentle touch. "You are right, James is it?"

"Yes, I am James, and this is Beth. We're not usually up this late, but seeing how things have turned out, we're here to help," said James with a grin on his face.

Beth glared at James, "Eager, aren't you?" she asked.

A.K. Baxter

Pillars of Matchstick Men

Beth tutted and stared at Athena waiting for instructions. "What do you mean?"

"Well... what are we doing next? I take it you know?" asked James.

"Here you go my dear, I have been holding on to this for a few years now." Athena opened her hands revealing the next scroll.

Beth leant in. "Oh no, not another scroll."

James took the paper and unrolled it to see what their next steps would be.

The paper said:

'To heal is to regain strength and power. In healing, I can grow. Bring forth the human and onto the next, to be free.'

Years ago, when the first reset undertaking began, four creatures of the nine were chosen to come to the human Realm and bring balance and choice throughout the realms. A game of matchsticks was played. Creatures of the nine gathered, each taking one matchstick. The longest pulled were given the title 'Matchstick Men', whose only task were to perform the reset for the benefit of the nine. It was Athena's role to be the watcher and guardian for all involved. Once the creatures arrived in the human realm, they were alone. With resets performed since the dawn of nine, this was the first failed undertaking.

For Athena, it was her most important role. As the daughter of a famous god. It was her personal goal to please the gods by leading the reset. She had always wanted a son and was destined to nurture many. But when the opportunity to lead the mission arose, she sacrificed her own dreams for the sake of humanity and the nine.

"Dear boy, James. I give you this scroll to decipher its meaning and I trust you both to bring back what is needed. But be warned, you are being watched."

James looked behind him and checked to see who was there, but only a dark empty field lingered.

Pillars of Matchstick Men

"What do you mean, we're being watched?" asked Beth.

"My sight is vast, and I can see, a bird of which is stalking thee."

"Oh, she rhymes too." Beth rolled her eyes.

"Just be aware and always look back," said Athena.

James moved towards Beth and whispered in her ear, "Don't suppose she means the pigeon?"

Beth laughed aloud, "You're joking right? If were being followed by a pigeon, then I'm shaking in fear."

"There was something off with that bird. Let's get going, shall we?"

"Got any ideas?" asked Beth, as she pulled out her batons and juggled. "Tick tock, tick tock," she sang in a little tune.

"I don't know, my brain is tired."

Beth dropped her batons to the floor and rummaged through her bag to grab the nougat bars.

"Here have some of this, it's pure sugar and will keep us going."

"Pure sugar? I haven't had any of this since I was 6 years old and thought I could fly down our stairs... it didn't end so well, my mum banned sugar from then on."

Beth snorted as she choked on her snack and reached for the nougat she gave him.

"Maybe I should take this back..." Beth moved in slowly, but before she could take it, he shovelled it in his mouth.

"Oh no," said Beth. "Please don't go weird on me."

"We'll be fine, let's get going. It's nearly 2am."

"Is it me or does time seem to be flying by."

"Yeh it does," said James.

"Ah ha! I've got it. We need to find something or someone that needs healing, like a cut?"

"You might be on the right track," said Beth. "My pet lizard, he accidently had his tail chopped off recently. My brother was performing a trick

Pillars of Matchstick Men

and it didn't go so well. I wonder if that would work?"

James reached into his pocket and reread the scroll.

"It specifically says it must be human. Unless your pet has some kind of shape shifting abilities?"

Beth face lit up with excitement, "I wonder ... we should try it!"

"Wait a second, we haven't got the time for this. It says human. There must be someone..."

"Everyone I know would make me perform 7 nights a week if they knew I left the carnival in the middle of the night. What about your family?"

"I've only got my mum and I'm not sure where she is."

Beth and James sat and the ground with their heads in the hands.

"There is my therapist."

"Really? If I can't check my lizard is a shapeshifter, then you can't have a quick therapy session."

"No, no, I mean she has a broken arm. We just have to somehow get her here and offer her to be healed?"

"That could work. Where does she live?"

James shrugged, he hadn't a clue where she lived, only that the office was a twenty-minute drive away from his house.

"Well that's no good if we can't get to her, plus it's in the middle of the night. It might look slightly suspicious."

"Oh wait, I have her business card, I wonder if her address is on there?"

James reached into his trouser pocket, the card now crumpled and folded numerous times. He lifted his jar of glow worms to take a closer look.

"It says, #94 greenwoods St, do you know here that is?"

"Not off the top of my head, no, but that's why I have a phone." Beth took her phone from her backpack and typed in the address to find on the map.

Pillars of Matchstick Men

"Ok so we are here, and Greenwood St is... about a twenty-minute walk away."

"That's better than a twenty-minute drive away; do you think we can make it?"

"We've still got five hours left before our time is up, so I'm sure we can make it."

Beth and James packed their things and looked toward Athena who rested upon the third lasting pillar.

"We'll be back as quickly as we can," said James.

"Be careful my dears, remember to always look behind you and stay safe. I will have my eyes in the skies."

Athena spun as she transformed into the owl, she flapped her wings and perched on top of the pillar.

Into the darkness and onto the streets, Beth and James set off on their journey to bring the third piece to reveal the next scroll.

"Look Beth, the second star is really shining now, that must be Athena's star."

Chapter 7

By candle light, only two were awake at this bewitching hour of the night. With the carnival in darkness, only whispers filled the stage. Merlot and Trent, the devoted clowns of the intrinsic carnival lingered, plotting.

The gods of the Guardian Realm have watched these two beings. Tricksters and Primagers walk among the human realm frequently, but over the

Pillars of Matchstick Men

years, the guardians have maintained a watchful eye on these two.

"We cannot let them get away with this," said Merlot as he twitched anxiously, like a nervous rat scouring for its last meal.

"Here, make the call. Nothing to lose," said Trent as he shoved the oversized phone into Merlots hand.

Merlot the clown was the taller of the two, dressed in oversized, bright white clothing. He seemed to be the decision maker of the pair. He dialled a number on the phone. Trent juggled to distract himself from the expected call. He balanced four balls high, on the top of his hunched shoulders.

"Hello Miranda, it's Merlot..."

"What are you calling me for at this hour? Is everything ok?" she asked.

"I thought you would like to know that Beth is not in her bed and is walking across the field as we speak. Quite frankly I don't think it is safe for children, especially girls to be walking out alone at night."

"OH, my goodness, definitely not. Thank you for calling."

The phone went dead, Merlot's eyes shimmered a bright yellow, then back to dark brown.

He rubbed his white-gloved hands together and snarled, "She won't be getting very far with the Mummy on her way."

But there was one thing the clowns did not know, with the pillars and the reset on count down, The human realm was stuck in limbo. A moment of stillness where nothing bad nor good could occur. A blanket of calm and rest was spread throughout their world. In fact throughout the Nine Realms. A time where even the creatures in the Intrepidus Gorge were restful rather than restless.

The human realm is the anchor of the nine, if this realm does not flow, nor can the rest. We are all connected. For the Guardian realms to function

Pillars of Matchstick Men

and protect all others, the nine must be in alignment.

The moment Miranda, Beth's mother, took action, her thoughts became lost and her mobility limited. Her will was that of rest and her memory erased as if she had taken a pill and—poof!—her recent conversation was wiped away.

Merlot cackled with laughter, a sound that spread across the field, past the pillars and into the streets, birds scattered from the wood.

All dressed in white, it seemed the night would give them away if they were to track Beth themselves. Yet they slithered from the carnival toward the pillars.

Trent sniffed the air with his flared nostrils, like a dog trying to catch Beth's scent.

"Nothing," said Trent.

"They couldn't have got far." Merlot whistled a pitch that only animals could hear.

"We need to get out of these clothes." Merlot dropped to the grass and rolled around, covering himself in grass and mud stains.

"Well come on then Trent, you can't risk being seen now." Trent followed suit and rolled around like a cockroach, enjoying himself far too much.

In swooped a pigeon and landed on Merlot's shoulder.

"Ah, Angarius, you made it, you will be our eyes. Changes are already happening and mere humans we cannot be."

Merlot held his hand out as the bird perched on his fingers. Feathers ruffled and eyes as white as their once-clean suits.

"Now go," said Merlot. The pigeon flew across the skies out of sight. "That should do the trick, we'll get their location in no time."

"What do we do now?"

"We wait, the humans are sure to fail, as always. The creatures of the nine are not who they once were, time has changed us, and so for them. I will stop at nothing. This earth will never see a reset again and we will stay bound to earth for eternity."

"But we've been here for too long already, aren't you getting tired of the same old, day in day out?"

Pillars of Matchstick Men

"You understand the alternative Trent, don't you?"

"Erm ... I think so." Trent scratched his head with a confused expression.

Merlot reached his neck up high to the sky. "The stars are too bright, without them these earthlings are sure to get lost."

Merlot tightened his white gloves.

"What are you doing?" said Trent with a gurgle in his throat.

Merlot stood still with his hands reaching up to the skies as he glared at Trent.

"What do you think I'm doing? Come on, catch up."

With his hands stretched out to the sky, he licked his fingers and mimed his way to try and wipe out the stars.

He wiggled his hands in mid-air, but with little effect. He closed his eyes with frustration and took a deep breath.

"Ok, come on, concentrate. It's been a while, but I can do this."

Trent stood with a gormless expression as he stared into thin air. He became more focused as a bird flew into his eye line, straight at him.

"Erm, Merlot..."

"Shh, I'm trying to concentrate."

"The... the bird is back."

Merlot huffed, irritated at his lack of powers.

"Ah, what ever happened to the human rights of magic?"

The pigeon landed on Trent's head, its claws mangled in his curly hairs.

Merlot pulled off one glove, as he failed to clear the stars, revealing only 4 fingers.

"Right come on then bird, tell me all." He turned around and noticed the mangled mess on top of Trent head.

"Oh, why do you always land in a heap of mess, for the twelfth time, this is not your nest. Just a silly man's head of hair." Merlot untangled the bird's feet. "Right come here Angarius."

Pillars of Matchstick Men

The pigeon rested on his gloved hand and closed its eyes as if it was sending information telepathically.

Merlot stroked the ruffles under its neck. "Well done my pretty bird."

Trent with excitement twitched on the spot and wafted around Merlot like a dog waiting for a treat. "Well, what did he say this time?"

"The horrible two are not far away, they are believed to be on the stretch of 11th Avenue and 59th Street, heading North among the houses."

"Right, ok, back to bed now?"

Merlot wacked Trent on the head with his juggling batons. "Of course not, we're going after them. With no sign of Mummy, it looks like it's up to us."

"So, we get to catch them? Then what?"

"Don't get too ahead of yourself now, first we must find out their plan. Without our magic we must use our brains, do you think you can do that?"

"Err, well I haven't used it in a while, but I'll try."

Merlot shook his head and muttered, "How is it I got lumbered with this idiot for over a century?"

The stillness has spread through the realms and the countdown to the reset is upon us. There can be no help for humanity, except for the four creatures that lay within the pillars. Not even the help of their fellow humans.

Time is a funny thing; it is only on earth, the human realm in which time is something. To the rest of the realms, time is fluid, time is space and an awareness of the now. Nothing can be saved for later, or to be done tomorrow. But on earth, time is curious.

The countdown is well on its way, the four pillars have experienced time unlike any other creatures of the nine. Only they can know the panic and frustration that time is not on their side. With only four hours to go and the odd Merlot and Trent on their track, Beth and James are running out of time.

CHAPTER 8

James peered left and right, quickly turning his head as though something made him jump. "Do you feel like were being watched?"

"You're only saying that because that Athena told us we were, I bet you anything if she didn't say it you wouldn't be acting like a wimp right now."

"I have you know I am being brave."

Beth snorted and choked on her own laugher, "You call this brave? It's just dark, and you've got a giant glowing jar of worms around your neck."

James sniffled as the frosty autumn air chilled his bones. Every word spoke through a cloud of steamy breath.

"Why are you like this?" asked Beth.

"Like what?"

"Well... wimpish?"

James didn't know how to respond. He clenched his hands, his knuckles turned white as he recalled his last holiday with his mother.

"You wouldn't believe me if I told you."

"Well... have you seen what we're doing? Last week I didn't even know your name, and now we're walking, talking, side by side in the middle of the night on a ridiculous mission to save creatures stuck in my local pillars I've played around my entire life. So, try me!"

James laughed at the thought. "This is all a bit crazy!" Beth nodded.

Pillars of Matchstick Men

"Well ... after my father died, my mother had to take care of everything. Life got too busy. She told me after a few years had passed, it was time for a holiday. She booked us a trip that she had won cutting out clippings in the newspaper, to Gibraltar. Mum was so excited I didn't really understand why, but we went. The plane was the best out of the whole holiday—if you could call it that."

"Isn't that just a big rock?"

"Yes." James grinned, "It's filled with cheeky monkeys but not very friendly people."

Beth's eyebrows raised waiting for a reason.

"What do you mean?"

"As I said, I was five and it was market day, Mum always told me to hold her hand or her handbag and so I held her handbag, thinking I was too old for hands. When a bunch of people walked towards us, as though a traffic light had changed, and all traffic directed towards us. I could see Mum's hand reaching down her bag trying to find my hand, but I had already been swept away into the crowds. I yelled, but it was too busy."

Beth followed James's footsteps as she walked by his side in silence.

"I wore stripy blue and green shorts with a t-shirt to match, we bought especially for the trip. I had my rucksack on filled with pocket money, binoculars and a book for the plane." James gasped to catch his breath. "I didn't see my mum again for two days."

"WHAT?" Beth's mouth opened in shock, she tried to keep her eyes on the pavement as they meandered down the path.

"A man found me, after 30 minutes of sitting alone on the side of the road, waiting for my Mum. He spoke Maltase and didn't seem like he knew any English. It was odd as many people spoke English." James rustled his hands into his coat pockets to keep warm. "I had no idea where I was, or how to speak their language. People looked at me but didn't seem concerned or kind."

Pillars of Matchstick Men

"Well that's not very nice." Beth rubbed James's back with conviction rather than just her usual sarcastic approach.

"So, what did you do for the two days?"

"Honestly... I don't remember, my therapist says I blank it out because it was too traumatic for me."

"Oh wow," Beth replied. "I would need a therapist too if that happened to me."

James chuckled and sniffled away his hidden tears.

"You... see a therapist? You would definitely give them a run around."

"What do you mean?" asked Beth.

"You're always so sarcastic, no one would ever tell if you were serious or telling the truth."

Beth made a short grumbling sound. "You're probably right," she said, "I've always laughed or made fun of everything."

"That there is your coping mechanism..." James said proudly, impressed he remembered something from therapy.

Beth rolled her eyes but knew deep down he was probably right. A fluttering up above caught her eye; it was the pigeon. The moment Beth looked up, it flew away. After a few minutes in silence along the darkened pavement, Beth broke the silence, "So how did you find your mum?"

"I remember waking up in a concrete building, no carpets or décor, just a room filled with concrete and there was a scruffy dog in the corner on a bristle like rug, couldn't have felt nice... and a blanket that must've been used to cover me in my sleep. I looked behind me, there was a blanket on the ground and a rolled-up coat, perhaps for a pillow? Whoever took me didn't have very much, just the dog I expect," said James, he wiped his nose with a tissue.

"You don't need to tell me if it's making you upset."

"It's ok, the cold air's making my nose run. I never saw who lived there, but I walked out of a blue and grey, heavy door, I didn't feel threatened, but I was scared and alone, not knowing how I got

Pillars of Matchstick Men

there or what was around. I was on the top floor of an apartment building, no one seemed to speak English, as I walked down the stairs clinging on to my bag, I remembered my pocket money, luckily everything was still in it.

There were mothers and their babies on the stairs, children chalking the walls, I felt I was in a somewhat safe place with mothers and children but none of them said a word."

Beth was silent as she stared at the speckled pavement.

"I was so confused. I walked out of the double doors to the building and the sun shone on my face, dust clung to my clothes. I was relieved when I saw the police station opposite me. That was definitely the best place I could've found. I remember the doors being so heavy. As I pulled it open the wind behind me slammed it shut, pushing me in. My mum was sat right across the waiting room from me, balling her eyes out, in the same clothes she wore when we got separated. She looked up at me as I called her. It was the best feeling in the world."

Beth's eyes welled up, she was happy for James, but it only made her think of her own relationship with her mother, or lack of it.

"Then what happened?" Beth sniffled.

"She grabbed me so hard and squeezed like she would never let me go again, I felt bad for not holding her hand and said sorry, but she looked me in the eye and said. 'Don't ever be sorry, this is my fault not yours. I am sorry.' We've never been separated since."

"Not even for a sleep over?"

"No, we've moved around a lot and haven't made many friends."

Beth grunted in agreement. "I've never had sleepovers either; no one wants to be friends with the circus freak."

James laughed, "Ah you're not too bad, freak perhaps, but aren't we all?"

Pillars of Matchstick Men

In an awkward silence, Beth checked the maps on her phone to make sure they were still going the right way.

"If the maps are right, we shouldn't be too far now, another 5 minutes," she said.

Since the moment James and his mother were reunited, they have not been apart since, except for school days and his therapy sessions.

An eerie sensation blanketed the sky as a flutter up above drew closer.

"Do you see that bird?" asked Beth. "It's like it's following us."

"What bird?" asked James.

"It looks like the one we saw in the tree back home."

"Bird is a bird, is a bird,"

"What?" said Beth.

"It's probably a pigeon." James adjusted his glow worms and rose them high, so he could see the path ahead, revealing a dead end. The only way they could escape was to take a sharp left down the darkened alleyway.

"You're kidding," said James.

"You have the glow worms; it was your idea to do this, so let's get on with it."

"I suppose that means I have to go first?"

Beth smiled and nodded toward to the alley.

A loud fluttering swooped above.

"Was that an owl?" asked James.

"Yup, something isn't right."

The owl swooped above their heads and tackled a bird that was behind them. James stopped in his tracks and caught a glimpse of the pigeon. The owl had the pigeon pressed firmly into the ground as it threatened it with its claws. The pigeon squirmed and was released. It darted away as fast as it could, cooing as if a signal spread across the winds.

"Athena?" yelled James.

The owl shook its feathers back into place and wafted its wings toward the children, flapping them fast toward to end of the alleyway.

"Do not stop children," said Athena. "More are coming."

Chapter 9

Merlot and Trent, not far behind, awaited for their messenger to arrive. But they did not expect to find him ruffled and flying loose winged. Angarius fled and carried the message without stopping, breathless and bruised.

Merlot shook his head as the bird dived into the grass below their feet. "Why do I do it?" Merlot tutted, "I should know by now, never send a retched bird to do a Diablo's job."

Trent let out a horrendous gasping sound as though choking.

"Are you alright?" asked Merlot.

"Yes, just... what you said... it was funny."

Merlot straightened up his white suit and pulled out a baton from its sheath on his back. He stroked it as though it was his prize possession. His eyes narrowed as a he concocted a plan. He ran his gloved fingertips up the baton and unhinged the tip, revealing a golden glow.

Trent nibbled the skin on his fingers, his batons were firmly attached to his sheath, his face sunk with unease. "What are you going to do with that? You haven't opened it in years."

"It is time, don't you think?" said Merlot. "We shall soon find out if this transfer works."

Trent gulped. "B ... but I thought they took it?"

"That's just what I told you, if you knew we still had it you would have blasted it away long ago. Unlike you, I'm not stupid. Transfers are our only

Pillars of Matchstick Men

way out, our vessel for travelling through the realms and my magic-safe. The gods would have to banish me with their bare hands before I lose my transfer," he said stroking his baton.

"But it's illegal, what about the humans? It's not made for their skin. Won't *they* find out?"

"*They*? They haven't been around for a century. I doubt they will notice us now. And any way, if we can't have our powers then this is all we have. Unless we can get our hands on an object from the realms, then this is all we've got. It's time things changed. Good riddance, I say." Merlot reached his fist into the sheath and took out a handful of golden dust. "We've been without for too long. If I release this, there's no going back. They will be warned, and they will come."

Trent scratched his head, "What do you mean they?"

"Not only is this my transfer, but the day before we left the gates of the gorge, I placed a magic signal inside," said Merlot. "Once opened the keepers will be called, just like Angarius. I have my allies."

"What about the dwarf? What if he finds out we stole his elixir?"

"He's probably long gone by now, they're known for their clumsiness, probably fell through a crack in the gorge. Nothing can stop my young looks, this isn't just dwarf magic!" Merlot flicked his wavy hair and pulled his gloves on tightly.

He scattered it through the night's sky, each golden particle flew like wild fire up higher towards the stars.

Merlot began to count down from, "5....4..."

Trent joined in with his gloves over his eyes, "3... 2...1..."

In that moment, the golden dust particles exploded releasing a wonderful chemical reaction, also known as fireworks. The sky lit up with vibrant colours. "That should get their attention," said Merlot. "The humans should never have been allowed to go this far, and as for the Primagers, well they're lucky it lasted this long."

Pillars of Matchstick Men

Merlot dusted his hands and pulled his gloves off his fingertips one by one, revealing his alien like hand. He clicked each finger, before covering them with a clean pair of white 5 fingered gloves. "My bones are still just as strong as they used to be," said Merlot.

Trent clicked his fingers too and said, "Yes they are, at least you still have all four of yours, I've got three left and I'm sure this one is on its way out." He flicked his index finger, as it flopped flat to his wrist.

"Well, that's the downfall for living for over a thousand years, something has to give," said Merlot. "Be grateful it's not your limbs, because if you don't be quiet, you'll be losing those too!"

Trent zipped his mouth shut with their sewn-on zippers, a prop used on stage, yet as real as it can be. For Pre-humans, Magic can only hold so much together. Over the years pain and patience has dissolved, and reinforcements are necessary. With zips at most seams, yet very much needed, stage makeup comes in handy.

Chapter 10

The children were not far away. The colours filled the sky and the explosions echoed through the quiet streets.

Beth and James gasped at the beautiful sight.

"Where do you suppose they came from?" asked Beth.

"Not sure. It is a bit late to be letting off fireworks isn't it? It's not even New Year's." James

Pillars of Matchstick Men

hesitated and knew something wasn't right. "We're not too far from her house now. We should go."

Beth still stood there in amazement. "Oh, let's stay for another minute, I've not seen fireworks in real life. We're not allowed them, good old health and safety."

James took Beth's hand and pulled her down the rest of the alley. "I really think we should go." He looked at the map one last time, to check they were on the correct path.

Beth's eyes were still glued to the night sky, the booms and shimmers hypnotised her entire being.

James knew he had to get her out of there, his hairs on his forearms stood up on end, a tell-tale sign for him that something was not normal.

"Oh, come on, what will snap you out of this?" He had to think fast. "Beth, look at me... we'll leave the alley way, so you can see the fireworks better." James nodded to get her to agree.

Beth tutted and her whole demeanour changed, her shoulders slouched.

"It's ok, I've got you." James tried to reassure her.

Beth dragged her feet through the alley and never looked down, her eyes locked onto the sky, in awe.

"We're nearly there," said James.

"More fireworks!" Beth clapped her hands with excitement as another bang went off and the sky lit up again.

Finally, they made it onto Greenwood Street.

"This is her road! We're close, keep your eye out for number 24."

James had hoped Beth would have snapped out of it by now, but her eyes were still fixed to the sky.

"I'll keep my eyes out then." James huffed and led Beth along the path.

Across the street was the number 8, then 10.

James knew they had to hurry, "The others could be close." he whispered to himself.

"Hey Beth, let's play a game. Whoever finds number 24 first, wins!"

Pillars of Matchstick Men

James gasped with excitement hoping to get Beth excited too.

"Yeah ok, race ya," she said. Beth sprinted down the road and acted out as though she was a spy, searching for the house with binoculars. James laughed at the sight. "What is she doing?" he whispered under his breath. "At least she's moving." James dashed after her until she halted in front of the number 24. "Well done, you won! Now to get her attention."

James's stared at the house and gulped as his nerves kicked in. "It's so quiet, don't you think?"

Beth rubbed her face and took out her drink. She was back to her normal self. "How did we get here?" She looked around the streets suddenly aware of their surroundings.

"Seriously?" asked James, "We ran, can't you tell... I'm out of breath."

Beth glanced around the street with no recollection of the past 10 minutes.

"Please tell me this is your friendly therapist's house?"

"I hope so, but it's very dark ... I've got an idea."

James walked up to the door and banged on it as loud as he could.

"That's your idea? This isn't working," Beth yelled.

"It has to." James did not stop. He kicked and knocked on every door. He ran around the house peering into all the windows, until a light turned up on the top floor.

"She's coming, quick to the front door." They both stood waiting for her to answer. The sky still lit with the fireworks, enough noise to wake up even those in a trance.

The light shone down the hall, her silhouette got closer through the stained glass window.

"Right, let me do the talking. Ok?"
Beth nodded.

"It's me Dr Sturgeon, it's James. I didn't know where else to go. We're being chased!"

The door flung open, and she put her spotted cloak around the two children, guiding them safely into her home. "Quickly, you'll be safe inside."

Pillars of Matchstick Men

A low-lit lamp filled the room with safety and warmth. James sniffed the air, a familiar scent wafted. "Those biscuits must be close by?" James asked Dr Sturgeon.

"Oh, yes. Would you like one?"

"Oh, no, err, I wasn't—"

"You must be hungry, and this must be Beth? You can both call me Francis." She took Beth's hand and clasped it with the other, giving it a shake. "How do you do?"

Beth coughed to hide her smirk and replied, "Tired and hungry."

Francis gave a sympathetic head tilt and said, "I'll go get the biscuits."

James's cheeks flushed. Beth tutted and said, "Boys, always thinking of their stomach."

"I was not!"

The floor was layered with a fluffy, pristine white rug. James looked at his shoes and noticed all the mud from the woods. He elbowed Beth and nodded to her shoes.

"Ah yes, but we can't stay long!" said Beth.

"I know. Let's just get her to the pillars and then hopefully it'll all be over."

They perched on the sofa, situated in the bay window, revealing a panoramic view of the outside street. Rain began to drip down the window.

Francis walked into the room with a tray filled with hot chocolate and biscuits.

"Oh, you didn't have to."

"Nonsense dear, it's late and you've had a shock. I'm glad you found my house. What ghastly weather out there, I don't know how I slept through the thunder."

"What thunder?" asked James. "It's only fireworks."

"Oh no dear boy, you must be mistaken, Giant Oak has band fireworks, you see our wood is a heritage site and kept safe, we don't want to risk burning it down."

"But we saw them, outside," said Beth.

Dr Sturgeon leaned in as though she couldn't hear her.

"What was that dear?"

Pillars of Matchstick Men

James looked at Beth, and shushed her, he tapped his watch, reminding her of the odd magic.

Beth glared at James. "Oh, perhaps you're right, we're just tired," said Beth as she reached for a biscuit and dunked it her hot chocolate. As she took a bite, a satisfied moan seeped from her mouth.

"How did you find my house?"

"Your business card, your address is on the back!"

"Oh of course it is. Jolly well done!"

Beth blew bubbles in her drink, amused by the dated phrase. She flinched as a shadow brushed passed her leg under the sofa. "Do you have cats?"

"No dear, they are my favourite animal, but I am allergic." Francis sipped her tea and said, "Now then, who chased you and why?"

James glanced at Beth hoping she would have an answer.

"You said you would do the talking!" whispered Beth.

James took a deep breath in and said, "We lied, no one is chasing us, we just had to get inside. You see something weird is going on and I didn't know where else to go. My mother is missing, and I am worried for her."

"Oh, you poor boy! where was the last place you saw her?"

"Well after my session with you earlier she dropped me off at the pillars whilst she went back to the market. She was supposed to pick me up, but I've not heard from her since."

Francis perched at the edge of her seat, with her glasses resting on the tip of her nose and let out a soft grumble.

"Where are you supposed to be, James?"

"I told Mum I would wait for her to pick me up by the Enigma pillars. Do you know them?"

"Yes, I do, I used to play there when I was a little girl."

James glanced at Beth and gave a smirk; his plan was coming together.

Pillars of Matchstick Men

Francis tipped the left-over biscuits into her handbag, slid her glasses back in place and said, "Right children, let's get your shoes on, were going to the pillars and we will find your mother!"

Francis clutched her umbrella and handbag on the other arm. "Can't be too careful when it comes to the English weather, rain or shine, an umbrella is very useful."

"I think this rain is about to stop," said James.

In a hurry, they all left the house, the lights still on. Francis popped open her umbrella and strode down the dark road.

James knew they couldn't tell Francis the truth; she would think they were mad and possibly have him sectioned, after all that is in her power.

"What's the time James?" asked Beth.

"It's 4.32am." He tapped his pocket watch, In shock.

"So, Dr—I mean, Francis, how is your arm feeling now?"

"You are sweet, it hurts, but the cast is helping it heal." Francis zipped up her purple, ankle length jacket to her chin and rubbed her hands together. "It's been a long time since I've been out this late. It's silent and quite eerie, really."

"You could say that again," said Beth.

James elbowed her, "Shh," he whispered. He didn't want to risk her saying anything she shouldn't.

"How far are these pillars then?"

"About twenty minutes," said Beth.

"Ah, ok. Well your mum could be on her way, so keep your eyes out and stay close to me."

The night skies now clear from fireworks, only a cloud of smoke lingered. The smell of sulphur remained.

"Oh, I do love the smell of fresh rain," said Francis.

"It's n..." he stopped himself before he gave anything away. James shook his head and muttered, "That's the fireworks she can smell."

"Something very odd is happening here," said Beth.

Pillars of Matchstick Men

Rustling and the sound of a lasso slicing through the air drew near.

Beth nodded to James and pointed to the sky, "We're being followed again."

James coughed to clear his nerves. "Francis, shall we walk a bit faster?"

"If you like dear, I'm not the most agile these days, but I can walk a tad faster."

James lifted his arm out offering it to Francis. "What a kind boy you are. Don't mind if I do." Francis hooked her arm into James's.

The cloud of smoke settled, ashes floated to the ground.

"What an odd smell," said Francis.

"Yeh, probably the storm," said James, trying to act normal.

"Oh, that's nothing," said Beth. "It's just my circus. It always smells like that after a night of fire spinning."

"Oo er," said Francis. "Sounds dangerous."

"It is." Beth glared at Francis, to give her a sense of fear.

Beth reached out to catch the ashes, showing her they were harmless, but as they settled on her arm they singed her sleeve, burning her hairs. Beth patted her arm as more ashes landed on her clothing. She rushed under the umbrella with Francis and James.

"Psst," she said trying to get James attention behind Francis's back.

James checked behind Francis and mouthed. "What?"

Beth pointed to sky and showed him her arm. The cotton on her sleeve melted a hole, her skin boiled and sizzled like an acid reaction. Her eyes welled with pain but she daren't show it.

Pillars of Matchstick Men

Chapter 11

Beth snuck under the umbrella and said, "Do you mind if I join you? I think I felt more rain."

Francis smiled and drew them both in close to her as she gripped on to handle and gave it a gentle twist.

"All will be well children," said Francis.

Beth snarled toward James, behind her back. James shrugged his shoulders and glanced toward the stars.

In that moment Beth and James became motionless, Francis unlinked his arm and stood in front. She giggled in a high pitch. "Ah, it still works." She rummaged through Beth's backpack and then James's pockets to check for any hidden lurchers that could obstruct their mission. She whistled through the gap in her front teeth, singing a happy tune. Lurchers hated happiness. Francis twisted her umbrella in her palm, it span faster as she muttered a song.

"Magic lies, and magic may, protect us from what comes our way. Magic of old has opened once more. But time has come just like before. Pillars must rise, the nine doth know, the clock is ticking and on we must go." With those words, the umbrella shot a thin ray of blue light from its top and disbursed like an exploding star, settling to the ground.

Pillars of Matchstick Men

She giggled in her peculiar high-pitched way. "Right, where were we?" She linked arms with the children and replaced the umbrella exactly where it was before. With her right leg back in the walking position, she twisted the umbrella slightly to the left, took a deep breath and nodded to the skies. In that moment the children carried on walking, but Beth noticed something had changed.

"Are you ok Francis?" Beth was dubious.

"Oh yes, just my leg. It's been walking for many years now and has taken me to some beautiful places, but tonight... this is special. I can't remember the last time I was out this late, the stars are out and it's just gorgeous."

Beth poked her head out from under the umbrella to check. "Oh yes, the rain has gone." She frowned at James, knowing something wasn't quite right.

"Got to love the English weather," said James. "Storm one minute and clear night the next."

Pillars of Matchstick Men

"Indeed, 'tis a strange thing, weather... Now then, did you see anything out of the ordinary on your travels this evening?" asked Francis.

James scratched his nose and checked for any birds in the skies. "No, not of sorts. Just the weather... yes... that's all."

Francis hmm'd, a pondering sound, as though she knew something was off. "Now, James, I have been your therapist for almost a year and I'm certain I know when you're telling the truth... or not?"

Beth snorted a laugh and said, "Sniffing out lies are my speciality, I've been doing it most of my life, having older brothers requires attention to detail. One wrong move in the carnival and you're a gonna." She glanced towards Francis and sniffed the air. "There is something off, lies I believe always come out."

Francis pursed her lips and drew her attention to James.

His cheeks flushed, the heat from his face emanated towards Francis.

"Well, I promise no matter what happens, I will help you find your mother. Nothing can harm you, as long as I have my trustee brolly, we are fine and dandy."

Beth giggled and latched on tighter to her arm. Francis glanced toward her and said, "You're a good friend to James."

"I hardly know the weirdo, but I suppose he's alright for a newbie."

"Ah yes, Giant Oak hasn't seen in many new faces over the years, or if they do, they never seem to last. I think it's all about population control."

James snorted as he choked on his own spit. "Population control?" he asked. "How do you mean?"

"I'm not one for conspiracies but it's like this town has its border control, surrounded by the woods."

James rubbed his arm as goose bumps spread across his body.

Pillars of Matchstick Men

"Yes. There is something odd about those trees." James glared at Beth as though suggesting that Francis knew something.

"Now, I have lived here my whole life and there's been no problems, until you come along. How do you explain that, James?"

Francis titled her head toward him, waiting for an explanation. He simply shrugged his shoulders and focused on his footings.

"We must be getting close, this seems to be taking forever," said James.

"I am sorry dear. It's my knee, it slows me down."

James tucked his arm tighter into Francis and smiled at her. "Thank you for coming with us."

She rubbed his hand and as she looked across the street, two shiny balls of light flickered, like a pair of headlights.

"Do you see that?"

James and Beth were eager to see it.

"Those lights?" said James.

"We are close," said Beth.

"Well what do you suppose those lights are?"

"It looks like my secretaries' cats' eyes at night time, it's something in their eyeballs that make them so reflective at night time. A sign of good night vision I believe, or so I read," said Francis.

"Full of wisdom, aren't you," said Beth in a sarcastic tone.

"Hmm, I wonder what that could be. What other animals can see in the dark?"

As they walked closer toward the lights, the pavement had ended, and the field was ahead. The remaining pillars stood in the distance like guardians of the night, watching the townsfolk.

"Is it me, or are there some pillars missing?"

James tried to change the subject and keep her unsuspecting for as long as possible.

"I think we're here, I know what those lights are," said James.

"Ethel. It's got to be."

"Ethel?" asked Francis, "Who's that?"

"Well, it's something you have to see to believe," said Beth.

Pillars of Matchstick Men

James and Beth pulled Francis toward to the pillars, desperate to get there before the time was up.

"Oh, it's only an owl, how lovely," said Francis, as Athena perched elegantly onto the Southern pillar. "I've never seen one this close."

James sniggered, "You'll see a lot more in a minute."

Out of the darkness stood Veranga, once invisible now a mere metre in front of them.

"You made it, welcome back. I trust you have solved the riddle and can make such an offering?"

"Err..." Stuttered James, "About that, we have brought a friend." He gently directed Dr Sturgeon forward in front of Veranga.

"What is this? What is he talking about?" said Francis. "I better not be part of some weird sacrificial business."

Beth chuckled. "No, we needed to get you here somehow, you see you may be the key to opening the next pillar, the next creature to reset Earth."

Francis let out a cry of laughter that echoed through the woods. "I must still be asleep, and all of this up to now has been a dream." Francis span her umbrella around in a state of delirium. "Hmm, I suppose as I'm here I may as well comply, what can I do for you?"

The tip of Verangas cane lit up an iridescent blue light, then dimmed back to its dark wooden tone. Veranga frowned and then twitched his moustache.

"Hmm, I must have forgotten it had a light, it's been quite some time since I've used this old cane of mine." He straightened up his suit, "Me lady, I believe only James and Beth can deliver you."

Beth nodded at James and said, "Come on, she's *your* therapist, let's get a move on."

"What am I supposed to do?" he asked.

"I don't know, it's got something to do with the third pillar, so come on."

Beth walked toward the pillar and sat on the grass by its side.

Pillars of Matchstick Men

"Err, right. Please Dr... I mean Francis, can you come here," said James. "We chose you to help you this evening, because I knew you had a broken arm and we needed something that could be healed to awaken whatever creature is in here."

Francis moseyed toward the pillar, gave a little knock and said, "Hello, Is any one in there?" She stroked the stone and traced the cracks. "Oh, well I suppose I can go back to sleep now."

The pillar began to vibrate, "What is that?" Francis asked. "The pillar is getting hotter and hotter, it's like a fire has started on the inside."

Beth and James looked at one another with confusion, they took a few steps back, as the pillar cracked and crumbled. Francis stood back with her brolly resting firmly into the ground in front of her. A red, hot fiery glow burst through the stone, blasting the pillar to dust and debris.

Chapter 12

The ball of light became smaller to reveal the wee winged folk, the fairies of the Healer realms. One's mischievous and led by fire.

"Ouch," A small voice cried from the teeny flutter as he darted toward Francis. James and Beth stood behind her, waiting for the riddle to play out. The heat forced her to the ground, James and Beth caught her and eased her down. The fairy rested his hands on her arm. "Ah, that is better," he said. The fire smouldered along her arm.

"What are you doing? Get off me, you'll burn me alive!" Francis screeched.

Pillars of Matchstick Men

"Are you not accustomed to my fairy magic? You have such a... familiar essence about you."

"I have no idea what you're talking about, but that feels better." She grinned at James and said, "It's healed, my arm is cool, and my pain has gone!"

"Yes, so has my burning body, thankfully."

The wee folk revealed its true self, an elder fellow, dressed in leaves for boots and moss for straps.

"Well, thank you for your help." Francis held out her hands for him to rest.

"Thank you for coming when you did. I am Rubrum of Fire. I've been trapped in that ruddy pillar for years. Your human realm must be in such a state for my aura to flame like that. I have not felt human suffering like it."

Veranga and Athena made themselves known and each bowed to one another with pride and joy.

"It's been too long Rubrum." Veranga held out his hand for him to land.

"How long has it been?" asked Rubrum.

"Well, almost a thousand years, give or take a few," said Athena.

"So that must mean... the reset wasn't completed? And now? Is it done? can we go back to the nine?" Rubrum beamed as he hoped it was all over.

"Not yet, wee folk, time is not on our side, with a mere 20 minutes until we're stuck, again," said Veranga.

Athena drifted forward with an elegant air about her. "Give thanks to these fine children. This is Beth and James. They have come at the right time," said Athena. "The Human realm is suffering and so are we. The nine are no longer flowing or in balance. If the darkness spreads, it will have nowhere else to go but up through the realms."

Rubrum's hands sparked with fire. "Are you telling me we've been stuck here for all this time and no one from the nine has come to help?" he asked, flicking the flames away from his palms.

"We are each assigned a role Rubrum, you of all should know this. We pulled the longest

Pillars of Matchstick Men

matchstick. A healer has its place, and as Matchstick men, only we can fix it."

Rubrum, once the leader of the wee folk, for two centuries, but there comes a time in a creature's life where they must sacrifice themselves for the good of the realms. His role of a Matchstick man, bound to only one job, to complete the reset of the nine. To reignite the realms power with a collective strike of the elements, all would be reset to its natural balanced state, to begin again.

Rubrum fluttered his red leafy wings, with a sigh of relief, the freedom and fresh air was a welcomed gift. He placed his hands up to his nose, and with three sneezes, his teeny body burst to the size a human. He wiped his nose and hands on the dried leaves he pulled from his pocket, but they turned to dust.

"Oh, looks like I'll be needing new stocks." Rubrum took Beth's hand and kissed the back with gentle caution as though kissing a spider's web. His lips barely touched.

"Thank you, lady, Sir. I have waited a long time for this day."

"Where did you get that gnarly scar on your face?" asked Beth.

Rubrum was silent, he froze as though in a trance. A few moments passed without a word.

"Um... hello?" asked Beth.

"He looks traumatised," James whispered.

"What could have done that to a small little faery? It's like someone scratched him from his scalp to his chin."

James wafted his hands in front of Rubrum.

"Oh, hello, sorry. I forgot about that. It happened... well I suppose that last day we were here. It was a lurcher, he had snuck onto my bird and attacked me. It must have been here to stop us from completing the reset."

"What's a lurcher? It doesn't sound very friendly," asked James.

"No, they're not," said Francis. "They are tiny trolls, shadows, that obey only one master, one who shows them power and magic first. They latch

Pillars of Matchstick Men

and drain those with trauma and negative thoughts. They enjoy the fear."

James gasped, "Francis, how do you know this?"

"I had to keep my secret, I can never tell who to trust any more. After they burned my mother at the stake by humans many years ago. My kind have to be careful."

"You're a...witch?" asked Beth.

"No, she's a Primager!" said James, "I knew there was something you were hiding."

"I'm sorry, I hope you can see that I hid it for your sake. You're littered with lurchers. My biscuits ward them off, but only for a short while." Francis passed James a biscuit from her handbag. "Eat, you will feel lighter."

James took a bite of the biscuit and let out a sigh. "That does feel better!"

"Yes, I can see a shadow has left, but more are coming."

"I don't like the sound of that!" said James.

Francis smiled, "Everything will be ok. I once had powers, but now all I've got is my nose for trouble and my trustee brolly."

Rubrum placed his hands on Francis's shoulders and said, "Together we can obliterate the lurchers. No more shadows or scars. We must reset!"

Rubrum brushed his hand across the left side of his face as sparks flew off his hand.

"My star shines bright, which means there is only one more task for you to do. The final pillar."

James and Beth looked to the lonely west pillar.

"Have you got a scroll for us?" asked James. Rubrum patted his pockets and rummaged through his bag. "Hmm... I don't have one. I'm not sure where you would find it." He glanced toward Veranga for an answer but received a shrug of his shoulders in response.

"We need the scroll to know what to do next!" said James, as he tapped his fingers together anxiously.

Pillars of Matchstick Men

Beth scrunched up her face and asked, "What becomes of the towns pillars once we break this one? These pillars have been the heritage of Giant Oak for centuries."

"If we can complete the reset, all will be well, a time set, and memories changed. Your world will be so much better." Veranga reassured her. "There was a time your world did not exist, instead it was attached to the Nine Realms—The universe at large. It was not until your choices began to affect the weight of the realms that it snapped and separated." Veranga clicked his fingers as though it was a quick event. "Yet still connected as one. The Human realm was your own creation. We completed Periodic resets for your safety and our own. All realms must be balanced for the nine to work together and thrive."

"You mean to tell me we are part of a magical universe?"

"Of course you are," said Veranga.

"Is there a way, say—for a person to travel to the realms?"

Veranga placed his hands on Beth's back and gave it a tap. "All in good time. First, you'll need a transfer, which only you can find."

Beth smirked at James, "Maybe there's more to the rumours!"

James took a deep breath and pulled Beth to one side. He looked to his watch and said, "We haven't got long left."

Beth looked at her wrist, "Where's my watch gone? I must have lost it on our walk."

"I'm sure it's fine, we're together anyway."

Veranga whistled and spun his cane around in boredom.

"We're coming..." said Beth.

They walked toward the western, final pillar.

"Well how do we open this one?"

The creatures looked at one another in silence.

"Someone must know?" asked James.

Veranga stuttered, "M... Maybe..." and waddled to the pillar, he tapped it with his cane.

"Nope, that didn't work."

Pillars of Matchstick Men

Athena shifted into an owl, with an elegant twirl and flew above the field.

"Something isn't right," she said. Athena darted from one length of Giant Oak to the other and back to the Pillar.

"We can't lose now, we're too close. There has to be an answer," said Veranga.

Francis twitched, scratching at her skin. "Can you hear that?" she asked.

"I can hear something, but are you ok? What are you hiding Francis?" asked James.

Francis searched around James and Beth, she pulled their pockets open and then rustled through the grass. "I'm just making sure you're safe, children."

"From what?" asked Beth.

"The lurchers, can't be too careful."

Veranga walked toward Francis and pressed his hands firmly on her shoulders. "I thought I recognised you. It's so nice to see you. Why here, why now?"

Francis rested on the grass, with her head in her palms. "I figured it'd be best to reside here, where I can help and do good, unlike in the other realms, where I am just another witch, another healer, a shifter. Please don't be mad at me, Veranga."

Veranga covered her hands and said, "Of course I'm not mad, humans have a choice and so do you. It's lovely to see you again. But why are you here now?"

"There has been a fore brewing for some time, twitchers and déjà vu, you know the feeling. Dark shadows that move. I can't sit back and not help. The lurchers are here," said Francis. "That cat you thought you saw, Beth, that was a lurcher, shifting in an out—spies for their master."

"Merlot and Trent!" said Beth. She looked at James. "The two clowns from the circus. It's got to be. The fireworks, the pigeon. They've been trying to get us all evening!"

"You're right! I knew there was something wrong with them. Not all there in the head or heart so it seems."

Pillars of Matchstick Men

"They're here." Francis looked up to the sky as the suns glow began to peak above Giant Oak.

"Time is ticking, children. We need to open the fourth pillar," said Veranga.

The sound of flapping wings awoke the dark night air, a murder of crows swept through Giant Oak. An eerie and rare sight.

Chapter 13

The crows swarmed in, darting and diving like it was their last meal. James cowered to the ground where a black bird pecked at his hair.

"Go away, you horrible bird!" cried Beth, as she waved her arms about. She ran toward James and shooed the birds off him.

"Are you ok? Get up, we need to run. They're not stopping."

James looked at Beth and said, "Thank you."

Pillars of Matchstick Men

Beth helped him up. "Let's go!" she said. They both fought the birds away.

Athena shifted into an owl, fearlessly defending the others. Veranga wafted his cane around, drenching the birds as they touched him. Their wings grew weary, one by one they huddled into a ball, with their claws tucked underneath and their feathers in tight.

"What's happening? What on earth are they doing?" asked James.

"I've never seen anything like it," said Beth.

"These aren't usual crows," said Veranga, "These are—"

"Lurchers," said Francis. "Their master must be close."

"Oh, not again," said Rubrum, "These pesky critters are getting on my flames!"

James walked toward a crow as it lay lifeless and still. He poked it with his shoe. "It's dead?"

"Why don't you have a closer look?" Beth egged him on. "You can do it." She winked at him with encouragement.

As Beth followed him, she picked up a crow. Just as he went to turn the bird over, she screeched, "CAW!" In his ear and wafted the bird at him.

James fell to the ground in shock. Beth stood still for a minute, waiting for his reaction. After a few seconds passed, James burst with laughter. A sigh of relief crept from Beth's mouth.

"I should have known you would do that!"

"I couldn't help myself," she said, as she leaned in to support him up.

Beth took a minute to view the surrounding chaos, black feathers littered the grass as though a wild animal had mauled them.

From the eerie silence, Beth startled at a shriek. James yelled, "HELP!" in a muffled sort of way.

Merlot and Trent had arrived. Standing behind James they forced him to the ground and gagged him with a white cloth.

Veranga dripped with water leaving a puddle around his ankles. The grass and leaves twirled around Athena revealing a goddess again.

Pillars of Matchstick Men

Rubrum's hand raged with fire, a symptom of protection and anger. Together they formed a circle around the Diablo's.

"Let him go!" demanded Veranga.

Merlot laughed and tied James's hands behind his back.

"You can't click your fingers this time. We didn't come all this way to just release the boy."

Merlot nodded at Trent and said, "Well go on then..." Trent mumbled a few sounds and bumbled towards James.

James looked at Trent with fear in his eyes.

"Leave him alone, he's done nothing to you!" said Athena as a tear dripped down her cheek.

Trent dangled the watch above his head, with a goofy smile and slowly passed it to Merlot.

"No reset for you! That was too easy." Merlot chuckled as he rewound the watch Veranga had given James.

"You can't stop the reset with one watch. Time can only move forward on this realm. A simple law of the nine, you should know that," said Veranga.

Merlot looked at Trent and bumped him on the head with his baton.

"No, but it can be stopped. Grab the other watch!" he demanded, pointing to Beth.

Rubrum raced Trent to Beth, hoping to stop him, flames sparked behind him. After being stuck in a pillar for a century Rubrum's' legs were still not used to gravity, and his pace was not quick enough. Trent threw Beth to the ground and whispered, "I'm sorry, but I need that watch."

"Well you can't have it! After all these years working with my parents and now you do this! How can you be so cruel?" asked Beth. "Surely, you've known all this time about the magic and the nine, yet you pretended to be part of our family for years, and now you want to destroy our world?"

Trent was speechless.

"Do it, Trent! Now!" yelled Merlot. "We haven't got all night!"

Trent checked her wrists, but the watch was nowhere to be found.

"It's not here!"

Pillars of Matchstick Men

Merlot screamed with frustration, his arms reaching for the skies as though asking for help.

Veranga walked toward Merlot and showed him his cane. Six singed spots decorated the edging. He rolled up his sleeves and rested the cane over his arm. Veranga held out his arms in front of him.

"Calm down now! Or you know what will happen. Poseidon was generous to me, and always takes care of his descendants. Do not test me."

Merlot snarled and took a step back, knowing that damage that his water power could cause.

"Why are you so desperate to stop this?" asked Veranga. "Do you remember the day of the guardian rising? We were all together looking forward to the next mission. As Matchstick Men we were a team, we were destined to fight together for the realms. I remember you and Trent. Both of you were just as excited as we were. To be chosen finally for something bigger than ourselves. Do you remember?" asked Veranga.

"You can't change my mind again. You and your high almighty guardians already did that for me. Giving us no choice."

"The guardians always do what's best for the realms, not individual promises. Look around you. Could you imagine what the world would become if these humans still had free power?"

Merlot scowled and rubbed his face in his palms. "But I am not human, I was powerful. I am powerful!"

"Yes, you are. But there would likely not be a human realm any more. A lot can change in a century, let alone a thousand years."

Athena snuck behind Merlot and Trent and untied James. She whispered, "It'll be ok. Stay with me."

"The Diablo's... they're part of the Matchstick men too? I knew there were six stars for a reason!" said James.

"Yes, they were chosen too, but they did not want for the same thing," said Athena, "They belong in the Intrepidus Gorge—a place gated and

Pillars of Matchstick Men

guarded by the giants and creatures of the night. It is a life of mirrors and doors. There, you must succumb to your darkness and shadows, heal and cleanse your soul. A process of a lengthy measure, perhaps many lifetimes."

James gulped. "That doesn't sound fun."

"It is a choice, see your darkness and overcome and accept it or be taken by it."

James frowned, "What are we going to do?"

Athena placed her finger on her lips to shush him.

Francis cradled Beth to make sure she was ok.

"What should we do?" asked Beth.

"I will think of something, don't you worry," said Francis.

Merlot shuddered, he raised his arms in the air and whistled a steady pitch. The birds rose one by one. Their wings flapped as feathers filled the air.

"Oh, not again," said James.

Merlot shouted, "Get her!"

Beth and James ran behind Veranga and Athena. Francis was on her own, an easy target.

Merlot raced toward her and tied her hands behind her back. With a small blade to her throat he threatened her and said, "Give me the watch or your therapist will be no longer."

James yelled, "NO! leave her alone!"

Veranga held him back and whispered, "It'll be ok. Stay with Beth."

The sun's light crept over Giant Oak, revealing a glistening through the trees, something that had not occurred since the Enigma Pillars arrival.

"Look," said Beth. "The sun is shining through the woods. Our time is nearly up."

"Why?" asked James.

"I don't know, but the darkness has gone."

Crows in the thousands swarmed them, the sound of caws began as though orchestrated. The birds flocked to the ground creating a wall between Francis and the others.

Rubrum's hands blazed, "Calm down." he tried to ease the flames. "You can't set fire to birds! That's not nice," he said to his hands.

Pillars of Matchstick Men

Athena span round, a whirlwind blew around her as she shifted into an owl. Her powerful air force blew the crows into the sky. Veranga ran as fast as he could to save Francis. But Merlot stood strong with the knife to her throat.

"Let her go, please. This isn't like you. If we fail the reset again, there won't be a human realm for much longer," said Veranga. "And the darkness will spread through the nine."

Merlot laughed. "You don't know me!"

Trent looked nervous, he whispered in Merlot's ear. "Put the knife down, I've got an idea."

"You... an idea?" Merlot grew angry.

Trent moved away and rummaged through the grass, "Got it!" he said to himself. He had found the watch, the time stood at 7.12am, minutes from failure.

"Are you going to listen to me?" asked Trent.

"Not now, Trent. I'm busy!" Merlot shooed him away.

Trent stared at the watch, he held the key to ending all of it. He placed it into his front pocket and waited.

"What's that over there?" asked Beth as she pointed to a blue glow on the ground.

"I'll go get it," said James. He carefully scurried along the grass as low as he could to not draw attention to himself. He picked up the rock which glowed an iridescent blue. "It's another scroll!" He ran as fast as he could back to Athena. "Look, this has to be for the fourth pillar?"

Athena cupped his hands and whispered, "Open it up and read it, but quietly."

James took the paper from the rock and unrolled it to read:

"Elementals gather, the pillars of Matchstick Men, North, East, South and West, together once again. Rise the last, rewind, reset and return."

In that instant the earth shook, and the pillar cracked.

Pillars of Matchstick Men

Beth dropped the ground in fear. "James!" cried Beth, "We've failed."

Merlot cackled with laughter.

The earth cracked and crumbled, and the ground sunk in on its self. Dust and darkness spread across the field. The light that finally glimmered through the forest now back to its cursed view. The crows flocked and fled Giant Oak. Their caws lingered with the dust.

Chapter 14

Merlots laughter roared as he pushed Francis to the ground. "I did it, nothing can stop me," he said with his arms reaching to sky as though waiting to be lifted to safety.

James rushed toward Francis, "Are you ok? I am so sorry I got you into this."

Francis rubbed her eyes and brushed the grip away from her throat. "My dear boy, it was inevitable. There is nothing that can change the direction in which we are to go. Have no fear

James." A tear dropped from her cheek onto his hand as he grasped hers.

"I'm not ready to die."

"Think of it as a chance to explore the Nine Realms, just another beginning. Hmm?" She smiled gently as to ease his nerves. "Perhaps your dreams have more meaning then we thought?"

"This can't be the end," said James.

Angarius soared across the dark skies, like a lap of honour. He darted for Merlot and tangled himself up in his hair, yet again. But Merlot stood tall waiting to be lifted and taken to another realm.

Veranga shouted across the winds, "You still don't get it do you! With a failed reset the realm will never be the same. They will be broken, out of alignment and your personal transfers won't work anymore."

"You're just trying to change my mind, but I have had enough. Trent are you coming with me?"

There was no sign of Trent.

"Hiding again, well your loss," shouted Merlot.

The final western pillar was gone, leaving a deep cavern in its place. The earth still shook as a groaning erupted from inside revealing a craggy two legged, 4 fingered, keyhole nosed giant. Athena flew to the giant and perched on its shoulder.

"What are you doing?" yelled Beth.

Athena flew into a key shaped hole in the giant's forehead.

James tapped Francis on the shoulder and stuttered, "W... w... what is that?"

"That is a giant, a fantastic giant," said Francis.

Veranga yelled across to James, "He is Speculo, or locally known as Speckles."

"Where on earth did it come from?" asked James.

Pillars of Matchstick Men

Veranga clambered the giant, as Rubrum flew past him. It was the largest climbing wall in the Scottish Iles. Using the moss and vines as rope to reach the giants head. Athena poked her head out of the keyhole and hooted, "In here."

The giant slowly spread his arms out wide, grinding rocks to the ground below.

James, Beth and Francis, ran as far back as they could to the edge of the field.

"Quick, under here kids. It's been fun while it lasted. I'm sorry I couldn't have been more help." Francis opened her umbrella and huddled them underneath.

"What good is an umbrella when it's raining rocks?" Beth sneered. "Thank you, James, you're a true friend, my only friend and it is in honour to die with you by my side." Beth placed her hand on her heart.

James sniffled and nodded, he rested his arm on her shoulder in acknowledgment.

"See you soon, Mum," said James, as he closed his eyes.

Speculo's fingers stretched out as he brought his arms back together and clapped his hands.

An echo of clashing boulders rang through the town. Darkness covered Giant Oak, a blue shimmering sheet of light stretched from the giants' head across the field, over the woods and into the towns. The light spread through the houses, into the schools, underground and into the skies. Darkness and a blue glow blanketed the human realm. Time stood still yet again.

Merlot stood frozen with a cunning grin on his face, with Angarius by his feet. Francis and the kids froze in time under the umbrella, surrounded by a large protective bubble.

In that moment the blue glow rippled across the Nine Realms, like a devastating wave. What would be left of the nine? The guardians of the realms sat on their pedestals in anticipation. It was out of their control, nothing could be done. The Matchstick Men were the only ones able to perform a reset each quarter of a million years.

Time had been ticked and the chimes of the healers had been rung.

In the town of Giant Oak, there were no lights, no movements and no sounds, not even the scratching of rats or the hum of the electricity.

Darkness seeped from the woods and sifted through the fields.

One light shone, a glimmer of golden light bounced through the forest. Trent had emerged from the wood, holding the light. Out of breath he collapsed onto the grass by Beth and James. His hand reached toward Beth's arm, he dropped the wrist watch by her side. Bursting a large bubble around them, as it popped and sprayed him in the face. They awoke.

Francis peered from under her umbrella.

"By joe, I think he's done it. Look, look!" She elbowed Beth and James. Beth rushed through her pack back and shoved her rope into Francis' hand. "Tie him up, it's our only chance."

"I think he's asleep," said Francis as she pointed her umbrella to his hands and zapped a bolt of light at him, tying his hands behind his back.

James turned toward Francis and said, "What was that light, just then?"

She winked at him with a cheeky smirk.

Beth picked up her watch and placed it on her wrist.

"The time... it's not yet 7.30am? What have you done?"

Trent covered in scratches and dirt gasped for air and said, "It's all his fault. I've been under his spell for years. I had to make things right."

James butted in, "B...but how did you change the time?"

"I didn't, I just paused it for a while. My transfer was in the woods and has been since I buried it when we failed the first reset."

"You have a transfer too?" asked Beth.

"Yes, my boot." He looked down to his feet, one a white, dirtied plimsoll and the other a black, moss decorated boot.

"I transferred the last of my powers and spells into my boot. It was all I had, and I buried it in the woods. You can never be too prepared."

Beth smirked. "James, what does your watch say?"

James flustered as he searched his clothes. I don't know where it is."

Trent stood up and rustled in his pocket, "Is this what you're looking for?"

"How did you...?"

"I have my ways." Trent smiled and saluted to Angarius as he flew overhead and perched by Merlot's feet.

"Angarius isn't a lurcher, he is my confidant, a comrade since Intrepidus Gorge."

James strapped the watch to his wrist and tapped the glass as the hands stopped moving.

"Well, what does it say?" asked Beth.

"Oh, there we go, its working again. It is 7.28am."

"Mine says 7.15, odd. It's always been a tad slow but not that far behind."

Veranga appeared in front of them, twizzling his cane. "I knew the Diablo's would try and stop you. The moment you mentioned the two men from your carnival when we first met, I had my suspicions it was the Diablo's," said Veranga. "I armed them once before, I would not make that mistake again. I set your watch slightly behind, just in case they tried to steal the time. As they are part of the Matchstick Men, their magic will work on objects from the nine, just like your watches. As long as one watch ticks and we set the pillars free, the reset is complete."

Beth let out a screech of relief. She looked at James and they both hugged Veranga.

"So, we didn't fail?" asked James.

"And the world hasn't imploded?" asked Beth.

"No, thanks to you, the human realm is all set to move forward again. The realms are ticking like clockwork. Pass me your watches and I will reset your time, so you can get some rest and begin your brand-new day."

With both watches in his hand, he stomped his cane into the earth. The skies rewound, from early morning to darkness, back to sunset.

"Now, let me introduce you properly."

The giant stood towering over the town, Athena and Rubrum rested on his rocky hand, they gave him a bow and glided to the ground.

"This is Speculo, prefers Speckles," said Veranga as he looked up his long-lost friend.

"Meet the fourth Matchstick Man, once the Gatekeeper to the Intrepidus Gorge. The keyhole into your own shadows. I am sure he will be grateful for the fresh air and the long stretch back to the gorge."

Veranga looked toward Trent and said, "Where is Merlot? You know you will both need to be sent back to the gorge. You must meet your shadow side and work in exchange for your forgiveness."

"Forgiveness?" asked James. "But he was the one that saved us."

"Indeed," said Veranga, "He does not need my forgiveness, or the guardians, but his own. Which may take some time."

Trent's cheeks flushed, as his boot shone bright gold, from the inside out. He stepped to the side.

"Merlot's here. Angarius dropped some sleepy dust on him. What will you do with him now?"

"If it were up to me, I would send him to the lower gorge and be done with him, but unfortunately it's not."

Veranga gave Merlot a light kick to wake him up. "Come on sleepy, game's over."

"Now the time still ticks, and we must keep moving, I cannot express my gratitude enough. You two are a joy to be around and thank you. We can all go home now. Your town will be back to its original state. You are always welcome to the visit the nine, any time." Veranga hit his cane onto his boot twice and gave James a wink.

"Transfer away we go."

Veranga, Athena, Rubrum and Speculo, walked towards the woods and disappeared into the trees.

James sighed, "Oh, shame we didn't have longer."

Beth tutted, "Well it was fun while it lasted, would you do it again?"

"NO!" said James.

Trent placed his hands on Beth's shoulders. "I'am ever so sorry. It was my fault your people got lost in the wood. When it was time to hide my transfer, I cursed the wood, so no one would enter. I did not realise the curse would allow people in. Rest assured it is undone and you have your woodland back." Trent bowed to Beth. "Thank your mum and dad for me. Been a privilege!"

Angarius swooped down and gripped Trent's shoulders, flying him away over the wood and into the nine.

Merlot still tied up, with his head to his chest in shame, he muttered, "I am sorry, you gotta do what you gotta do. I only wanted my powers."

Francis nodded and said, "I understand, I've never let my power out of my sight, I suggest you do the same."

Francis untied Merlot, he twisted the end of his baton three times, and evaporated inside it.

As the sun rose above Giant Oak, the rays shone through the trees, lifting the heavy darkness.

Pillars of Matchstick Men

James reached into his pocket. "I knew I still had some left." With His hands filled with acorns he gave some to Beth and said, "You know what to do."

Where each pillar stood, remains holes and dirt, a perfect spot for four giant oaks.

"Good job done." Francis huddled the children next to her and said, "Right, shall I walk you both home?"

James stood still in his tracks as a familiar silhouette stepped over the hill.

He smiled and said, "I think I'll be ok, thank you."

"Is that your mum?" asked Beth.

James nodded and gave Beth and Francis a squeeze.

"Don't be so daft, I'll be seeing you again soon," Beth said as she gazed toward the circus, the lights shone below the hill, she smiled with relief. "Come meet my parents, they will like you. Maybe you could take over from the Diablo's?"

James smiled and said, "Me?"

Beth nodded with confidence.

The first morning of the reset was no different than the one before and humans were none the wiser. The magic and the myths that were set in these towns still lingered, but the proof was hidden. It's only a matter of time before the next generations unlock even more power than the previous.

Humans... are the ones who have brought down the weight of the world and are the only ones who can fix it. Rumours of robots are heading this way to do your dishes and fold your laundry, run your stores and be your teachers. Who will be the majority for the next reset, humans, robots, goboids, or perhaps the Nine Realms will become eight?

The End

Next in the Nine Realms series
Book III to be released in 2020:

Residing in the Turner Realm are the naguals,
shifters and creatures of the night— No place for
human smalls.
A young nagual, named Jaka, dreams of an
education on the human realm, away from his
shapeshifting family.
With a nose for trouble, something has raised
his hackles. Children are missing throughout the
school, and so are their souls. Jaka and friends
must travel the realms to stop them taking over
Winterborne Academy.
For help can only come from the source of the
chaos caused.

Contact the Author:

By email:

Mountwillowbooks@mail.com

Akbaxter@email.com

Keep up to date with events, book signings and new releases, via Social media.

Sign up for A.K. Baxter's newsletter for regular updates and giveaways, including free books and discounts, events and activities.

https://anniekbaxter.wordpress.com/

https://www.facebook.com/AnnieKBaxter/

For information on Annie's adult and children's meditation course, go to:

https://www.facebook.com/mindfulmammas

E-book coming soon.

Books by A.K. Baxter

-Nine Realms series

1. For Goblins' Sake
2. Pillars of Matchstick Men
3. Title to be released summer 2019

The Nine Realms series feature three stand-alone books, which includes one more to published in the next year of 2020.

A brand-new and exciting fantasy universe coming up next for A.K. Baxter. Join Annie online for more information and book updates, meet the author and book signings.

If you enjoy the Nine Realms series, don't forget to leave a review on amazon or social media. The support is truly appreciated and helps reach a larger audience, and hype for more exciting books.

You can find the first book in the series on Amazon or contact the publisher or author for a signed copy.

Nine Realms: 'For Goblins' Sake'
https://www.amazon.com/dp/1775205304

A.K. Baxter

Pillars of Matchstick Men

A.K. Baxter

Pillars of Matchstick Men

A.K. Baxter

Made in the USA
Middletown, DE
13 July 2019